Eos of the Infernal

Aritra Chakrabarty Sengupta

ISBN 978-93-90040-24-7
Copyright © Aritra Chakrabarty Sengupta, 2020

First published in India 2020 by Inkstate Books
An imprint of Leadstart Publishing Pvt Ltd

Sales Office:
Unit No.25/26, Building No.A/1,
Near Wadala RTO,
Wadala (East), Mumbai – 400037 India
Phone: +91 969933000
Email: info@leadstartcorp.com
www.leadstartcorp.com

Editor: Ateendriya Das Gupta
Cover: Ashwini Jadhav
Layouts: Kshitij Dhawale

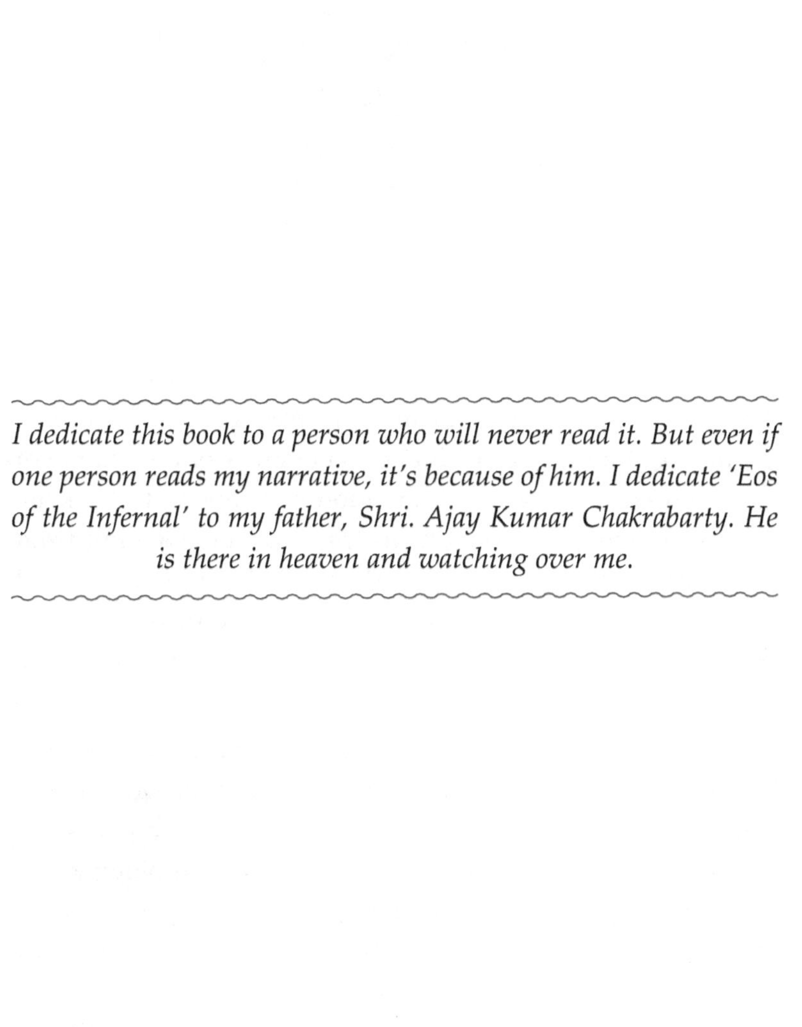

I dedicate this book to a person who will never read it. But even if one person reads my narrative, it's because of him. I dedicate 'Eos of the Infernal' to my father, Shri. Ajay Kumar Chakrabarty. He is there in heaven and watching over me.

ABOUT THE AUTHOR

Born in the magnificent and chic township maintained by the 'Steel Authority of India' in Kulti, West Bengal, Aritra had a fulfilling childhood. She did her schooling from Assembly of God Church. During her graduation, she moved to Kolkata. After completing her B. Tech in Chemical Engineering from the University of Calcutta, she shifted to Surat, Gujarat, and started working with Reliance Industries Limited. Since the later part of 2012, she has been in Mumbai, where she stays with her husband.

Though a techie by profession, Aritra has always been in love with words. Hence, writing comes naturally to her. She has a website—www.talestotell.online—where she pours her thoughts and voices her protests. She is a regular blogger and loves travelling. She is an avid reader. Fiction appeals to her more than any other genre, as the characters become a part of life. Her love for fiction and her passion for conveying her thoughts drove Aritra to write her first novel, *Introspection*— an evocative journey of a young couple, which leaves us with many questions and appeals to society to alter its parochial norms. It was published conventionally by Wordit Art Fund, and the manuscript was amongst the chosen few out of five thousand odd entries.

The book was launched on 11 December 2017, and the event was graced by eminent personalities like Mahesh Bhatt, Dino Morea and Bikramjeet Kanwarpal. *Introspection* has received great reviews.

Makeup, hair and styling : *Nivedita Sen*

Photography: *Tathagata Sarkar*

ACKNOWLEDGEMENT

I thank you, dear reader, for choosing my book. I hope you have a wonderful experience reading it.

Writing a story is a beautiful journey. But it has its emotional ups and downs. My heartfelt thanks to my husband, Avishek Sengupta, for holding me together through this turbulent voyage and helping me come up with an apt name for my book.

A book is a reflection of thoughts, and the stability of my mental thoroughfare is ascertained by my family. I thank my mother, Smt. Aloka Chakrabarty, for having faith in me. On days when I felt lost, her encouragement meant a lot. Thanks also to my mother-in-law, Smt. Rupali Sengupta, and my father-in-law, Shri. Dilip Sengupta, for being so supportive.

I thank my lovely sisters, Soma and Rimi; my brothers-in-law, Dr Subrata Chattopadhyay and Shri Saikat Mukherjee; and my adorable nieces, Sohini and Tiyash, for being a constant source of gaiety and encouragement.

Last but not least, I sincerely thank Leadstart Publishing for this opportunity.

CONTENTS

CHAPTER 1

Mumbai, India, 7:30 hrs

"Chameli … Chameli!" I could hear it, or rather feel it, like several pins piercing my eardrum.

I hate my name.

My responses were numb, my body parts were not my own. But my ears did their job, though I wished that they wouldn't.

"Chameli! You lazybones! Do you know what the time is? It's 7:30 already, you thick-headed creature. When do you plan to pull yourself out of this mess you call your bed?"

As the blabbering recommenced with amplified vigour, my oblivious state created a muddled version of it, which prompted me to change my sleeping position and face the wall. As if turning my back to my reality would save me from the reverberation.

"All right, I'll spare you ten more minutes to laze. But remember, by the time I call the other girls I want to see you up and about." And this time it was an order—harsh and strong. I perceived that I had to abide.

However, even in the bewilderment of sleepiness, I knew that Nanda Masi would take considerable time to return to my dingy corner, and so, I felt relaxed. The inner calm brought back the dying remains of my incomplete slumber, and I could feel myself being engulfed in oblivion.

* * *

"Era … Era …!" I was dreaming. It was a different voice—but familiar. It was not harsh, like Nanda Masi's. It was my mother's.

"Era! Get up now. Your father will leave for office in thirty minutes;

I want you to get ready. Era … Era … are you listening to me? He will drop you to school … Era!"

"Ma, five more minutes please," I pleaded.

"No, baby, your father has some important commitments; he has got to rush to work. Get up, lazy bones! Take a shower and brush off drowsiness. Era … Erawati … my baby, go run … Appa is waiting for you." The voice felt like water on my drought-stricken soul. I felt my yearnings transcend into divine peace.

I heard her footsteps retreat from my room. My room—a little haven with delectable cream walls! I was always in awe of my snug space. With posters of my favourite cartoon characters generously occupying most of the walls, it was a corner where peace, creativity and intellect struck me with full might. I would often get up early, to watch the rising sun, a magnum opus that could only be beheld from my expanse in the entire house.

"See what I have prepared for breakfast today, your favourite—dosa and yummy coconut chutney. Get up now, Era." Ma continued from the kitchen, trying to bribe me into getting out of the bed.

"Yes, Ma."

✳ ✳ ✳

As I was struck in the dwindling lanes of memory, my oblivious self-suffered the unsanctified blows of reality and my eardrums were pierced again, mercilessly this time.

"Chameli?" It was a query laden with anguish and shock. "You are still in bed?" Nanda Masi threw her hands up in desperation, bewildered and angry. "This is how you girls instigate the evil side in me to surface … and they say I am ruthless." Saying this, she bent down and pointed a finger at my face. "Didn't I ask you to get up before I return to your room? Didn't I … answer me!"

I nodded like a scaredy-cat.

"Then why are you still in bed?" There was a subtle warning growl, and before I could react to that vexed utterance, the side of my head facing her received a resounding slap. The drowse clouding my senses vanished into thin air. What remained was an echo of despair and untamed emotions flowing out of my melancholy-laden eyes. I sat up like a spring doll, and with my right hand on my hurt head, I looked at her in dismay.

"What … what are you staring at? You invited this treatment, didn't you?" Nanda Masi spat out. "How many times do I need to ask you to get up? Are you a princess, huh?"

I didn't want to talk; the pain aroused some unwanted dizziness in my head, so I just continued to scrutinize her with my questioning eyes. The hand on my head felt the roughness of my hair, which had also acquired an unhealthy reddish tinge. As I sat cross-legged with my floral-printed cotton frock on, I could see some bruises on the exposed parts of my body.

"Stop ogling at me like that! Your fake innocence won't evoke remorse in my heart. Do you understand?" Nanda Masi rolled her eyes at me and then glanced at the flashy watch on her right wrist. "And my princess, you don't have much time left," she sneered. "Running water will be available for another half an hour. Go run, take a shower and put some shampoo on your hair … it looks horrible."

Her work was to order, but executing those orders was a mammoth task for me. My head was reeling with the impact of the slap it received. My seventeen-year-old self was voyaging on the rough sea called life. Malnutrition, abuse, and unhygienic living conditions were like sharks around my demure self, opening their predator-like mouths to gulp down the remains of dying hope. I was neither entitled to sick leaves nor love and care. In fact, I had discerned that I wasn't even entitled to be myself anymore. My life wasn't mine at all.

"See how much time you have wasted procrastinating? Don't force me to punish you!" she roared.

"I … I don't feel good today," I stammered. Although I did not expect an iota of compassion, my inner self urged me to assert myself.

"Hmm." She scanned me from top to bottom, "Your habits are obnoxious, you don't bathe regularly nor take the medicines I ask you to … what do you expect?"

I couldn't reply, choked in abhorrence.

"Now go and take a bath. You smell awful," she gave me a look of disgust. "We will go and see a doctor, okay?"

I could recognize the undertones and knew that we would *never* go to any doctor. We would just wait for an NGO to conduct a complimentary medical check-up for the brothel girls. A bitter smile formed on my lips, which she didn't notice, fortunately. Carrying my dirty towel and a poker face, I walked out of that room. I had no choice but to follow her orders.

There were striking incongruities between my room back home and the one in the brothel. While in the former, energizing crimson rays found their home, the latter was dark and sultry, with the paint woefully peeling off the walls. In the morning, the rays of the sun struggled to reach the dark corners, fighting the humongous number of clothes hanging in the open corridor. Even the mighty rays suffered dolorous defeats at the hands of shame.

The curtains of my drab territory were stained and smelled of stale organic fluids. One could never make out their original colour, for there was a riot of hues struggling to co-exist. However, a dirty green tinge dominated. I refrained from touching them.

In my ten feet by ten feet prison of humiliation, there was a creaky bed too. In fact, all the rooms had similar ones. And it was quite a pandemonium at night.

My cupboard was carefully segregated. One segment had all the articles that I despised, and another was a sack full of nostalgia. The former included my tacky attires—flashy, cheap make-up items, some bottles of inexpensive liquor and glasses, and a strong perfume. The other section held clothes that soothed me and reminded me of my identity. It also had some bits of paper—tattered pages of my life.

There were two bulbs in my dingy corner, one red and one yellow. We were asked to keep the red light on at night. It camouflaged the shadiness of the rooms, in its lusty embrace.

CHAPTER 2

All the girls stood anxiously around the tap area. Running water was a luxury here. In our lives etched with internal conflicts, these girls had learnt to find solace in the little joys of life. The only person playing hide and seek with reality was me. Inevitably, I was late.

As I struggled to bring myself to face the hideous reality, I heard a familiar voice. "Chameli! You hardly have twenty minutes. What are you waiting for?" asked Nilofer, my co-worker.

"Yes, I will brush first and then take a bath," I replied. Walking over to the tap area, I grabbed my pink toothbrush. Its bristles were hard. Not the kind I liked. I remembered the comfort of using the soft ones that my father used to buy for me.

Drowned in my thoughts, I gazed around clumsily while brushing and recalled the bathroom Era was used to. That beautiful, pink tiled restroom had a huge, round mirror. One of the few expensive interior decoration pieces, Ma had insisted to buy. No wonder, she maintained it with all her heart. Then there was the tiny, sky-blue toothbrush holder. It was my favourite.

As I brushed my teeth, my eyes fell on my own reflection. The water on the floor of the tap area gave me the opportunity, which the mirror-starved bathroom walls couldn't. I stared at myself, aghast. Era was lost, Chameli stared back at me. And in that very moment, I wanted to perish into nothingness.

I had changed a lot. My skin had turned a shade darker. The effect of cheap quality make-up was evident from the uneven patches on my youthful face. My hair was frizzy and reddish. Eyes, where were they? They were concealed in melancholy. The gleam, the life, and the love had vanished for good. I wondered if they were the same pair of eyes that Ma thought resembled Goddess Durga's.

Around four years ago, we had visited Kolkata during Durga Puja. The city was overflowing with tangible luminescence. And in one of our pandal-hopping excursions, as I stood awed by the beauty of the Goddess, Ma had suddenly exclaimed, "My Era's eyes! Aren't they just like Ma Durga?"

"Chameli, go. You don't have time to sit and think all day," Nilofer reminded me. The reality-check was back-breaking. I gave her a look and made my way to the bathroom in despair. She smiled at me.

Nilofer was my only friend and confidant in that world of filth. She was unlike Rosy or Queen or the others, and our thoughts were quite in sync. Both of us hated the place, the work, and Nanda Masi. We craved to watch television and read newspapers and gain knowledge, even in that darkening penury. After all, back home we both were pampered kids and so, Nilofer and I always had something common to discuss.

But the other girls saw our shared bond as snobbishness. They believed that we were opposed to them; since we had had the privilege of education. But the reality is that no relationship is possible without some shared interests.

For the other girls, the brothel and its darkness were their home; they had accepted that. But we couldn't. Getting themselves caked with make-up and standing by that drab lane every evening—that was what their lives meant to them. I don't condemn or belittle them; they likely never had the fortune of living a better life. A juxtaposing world did not invoke pain in them, simply because it did not exist. They didn't know any better. So, they were different from us.

By the time I went inside the small bathroom, the water

pressure had reduced. I knew I had to be quick. Placing the bucket under the dying flow of luxury, I started to undress. Then, I gradually allowed the chilled water to embrace me, the initial frostbite was always tough. But soon my body relaxed.

An unused sachet of shampoo was lying on the floor. The soap bar in a metal soap holder was breathing its last. It was common to all and seemed to need a bath more than I did. I obliged and smiled trying to gauge the repercussion if Nanda Masi ever knew of the wastage.

Drowned in my thoughts, I slowly sat on the floor and rubbed myself with the soap. I also washed my hair. However, my skin did not feel like my own. Ever since the indecency of my occupation had touched me, I had felt a layer form on it. I never got to touch the real me. And as I closed my eyes and poured water, which trickled down my encrusted self, the unsettled memories came back to me. I was neither soothed nor cold. I just wondered if I was alive. Then gradually, the feeling changed. I felt the droplets caress my body.

✻ ✻ ✻

The water was lukewarm. I could hear Ma shouting from outside the bathroom door and knocking it slowly. "Era, come out now. You will catch a cold, Appa is waiting, Era."

I could hear another voice too. First muffed, then clear, it was Appa. "Nandini, you are really spoiling Era. See, she does not listen to anyone. You told her that I have work, and still she is taking her own sweet time," he remarked, trying to sound angry.

"I spoil her?" Ma yelled, agitated. "What? Look who is talking!"

"What do you mean?" Appa responded, but the conviction in his voice had already started to falter.

"Mr Iyer, the only person who is spoiling Erawati is you! We Bengalis are not like that. We … we are strict people!"

"Oh come on, Nandini. Bengali moms are famous for spoiling their kids—"

Ma didn't let him finish. "Oh, so you mean my Ma has spoiled me, huh?"

I could picture the plethora of expressions on her beautiful face. I couldn't hold my laughter, imagining how Appa must be cursing himself silently for falling prey to his own habit, of uttering the inappropriate things in unbefitting situations. I had already gauged the tone and knew that a battle of words was about to begin, and I couldn't wait for the friendly fire to ignite.

My father, Mr Suresh Iyer, was a Tamilian and my mother, Miss Nandini Mitra, was a Bengali. Well … a proud Bengali to be precise. Theirs was a love marriage. Although Ma had adorned the Iyer surname with grace, she remained a hardcore, fish-eating, book-reading and music-loving Bengali. Often, the four walls of our little abode of love witnessed these wars. The war between Tamil righteousness and Bengali uniqueness! And the lingual and cultural contrast emerged hilariously during their arguments. Nevertheless, they shared a magical bond. Quarrelling like kids, romancing like honeymooners, maturely handling their parenthood—they exemplified the beauty of togetherness.

But it wasn't simply a happy journey for them, as their families never approved of their marriage. However, they were adamant, and Appa made his belief very clear to everyone. He believed it was not correct to implant invisible walls of caste, creed, culture, or colour between likeminded people. I was blessed to be their child and the living testimony of their commendable grit.

✳ ✳ ✳

"Chameli … Chameli!" I could hear Nilofer's voice and her frantic knocks on the weak bathroom door. Thankfully, even in my stupor, I had the senses to quickly wash off the soap and the shampoo.

"Um, yes, yes! I am done … just a minute!" My dream world was my sole space for solace, and whenever my rendezvous was interrupted, I felt lost, unsure of my existence.

As I walked out of the bathroom, I noticed faces staring at me, with expressions varying from inquisitiveness, irritation to agitation. But the experience wasn't new; in fact, I was used to it. So completely ignoring the stares and glares, I walked over to my room, clumsily holding on to the towel, the only piece of clothing to cover my body.

Nilofer was leaning on the door of her room, which was next to mine. She smiled at my ineptitude.

"Why can't you call me Era, huh?" I asked, irritated, and continued walking. It wasn't the first time I had asked her that question.

"Chameli …" she started with a grin.

"Era … Erawati is my name …" I snapped.

"Go dry yourself and dress up. We will talk later."

I was vexed but I went inside my room without further argument. To display my anger, I closed the creaky green door with a loud ceremonious thud. Though I couldn't see, I could sense Nilofer's amused smirk. The very thought angered me more.

I dropped the towel and stood in front of the mirror. My demure self and my nakedness both looked alien to me. There I was, around five feet and two inches tall, lean, with dark and searching eyes. The towel lay scrambled at my feet, like a beheaded warrior; it was dead with shame. My lacklustre eyes were scanning my frame from head to toe. It had almost become a ritual after bath; perhaps each day I was getting more accustomed to the un-familiarity of my body.

Before I came to the hellish abode of flesh trade, I had never felt the need to shamelessly peer at my nakedness. Except one time, in what I recall as my debut encounter with my femininity. My mother had got me a pretty red frock on my sixteenth birthday. I remember closing the door of my room, undressing and admiring my growing womanhood.

But that was a different me, with no resemblance to the girl who stared at me aghast from the dirty mirror hanging on the wall of this brothel room. The brutal self-scanning paused a little above my right knee. There was a bluish patch, a bruise.

"So that's my new piece of decoration from last night's gig!" I thought aloud, then bent down to touch it, and twitched as the pain flared. In a flash, the memories of the nights I had spent in that room flooded my mind, and I pushed them away with all my might. I hated recalling those dark nights—spent amidst sweat, cheap fragrances, and unknown dark shadows with slurred speech and scavenging hands. I immediately felt claustrophobic and nauseated. Every night brought with it a different tale, a different pair of ugly hands. But one thing that never changed was the derogation. It was the only constant in my colourful life of changing partners, or rather, customers.

I laughed in derision. Thank God, the door was closed, or Nanda Masi would have labelled me insane and deported me to the mental asylum. After all, I was not a very saleable item in her shop. I was resentful and unattractive.

As the array of thoughts passed my mind, I realized that I had been staring at myself for too long. Almost immediately, my senses urged me to cover myself. I put on the printed cotton maxi. Then I dried my hair with the towel and prepared to open the door. But before I could do that, someone banged on it hard.

"Chameli ... who the hell do you think you are, huh?" asked the voice, anger oozing out of every word she uttered. It was Rosy, I discerned from the timbre.

And before her cursing recommenced, I flinched at my carelessness. "Oops, I left my frock and under-garments on the bathroom floor," I muttered. It was not the first time.

Although completely aware of the fate that awaited me on the other side of the door, I had to open it and as soon as I did, Rosy snarled at me. "Again! Again you have left your clothes in the bathroom. Every day you make the same mistake. Sometimes I am not sure if you are forgetful or if this is deliberate! And who is responsible for collecting them? Who will wash them, huh?"

"Rosy, I am. I ..." I was struggling to get to a logical explanation. Declaring myself sick might help—but every day? No, it wouldn't work.

"What?" barked the self-proclaimed monitor.

"Rosy, I am sorry. I don't know why I forget. Don't worry, I will wash them in the evening, and ..." I could not finish.

"And what? If you spend time washing clothes in the evening ... how will you work? Besides, it is irritating to see your clothes lying on the bathroom floor every morning. You know it is my duty to clean it, right? I don't have the luxury of lazing around like you ..." She bragged on. I was barely listening to her anymore.

Work? What work? We are bloody commodities in a showroom. In my mind, I was laughing painfully at the conviction with which she was describing her employment, her life. Strange! Was it really that normal for her, to sell her body every night?

After a few moments, when I tuned her in, I heard her saying, "It is enough now! Mend your ways or …" It was a not-so-subtle threat that she would complain about my irresponsible behaviour to Nanda Masi.

"I am sorry. I will be careful." I said this primarily to shut her mouth. It worked, almost magically. She stopped blabbering, and her expressions mellowed.

"Fine!" she muttered and walked away.

As she trudged towards her room absentmindedly, taken over by a strange whim, I suddenly called out "Gauri!"

She stopped, as if the name had exploded like a bomb inside her head, numbing her senses and freezing her movement. Hesitantly, she turned back; there was a visual alteration in her expressions. I could not get what they meant. Initially, I thought she was touched, just like I would have been if someone addressed me as Era. But I was wrong. She was angry. "Don't call me that!" she said coldly. "I am Rosy … and that is my only name, only identity. Don't you dare!" She turned away again, more swiftly this time.

"But … don't you miss being what you truly are?" I asked without thinking.

She turned back to look at me with palpable anguish, and for the first time, I saw tears in her eyes. But she resented showing them. It was also for the first time that I could see beyond her forced sleaziness and was surprised to note that she was indeed beautiful. Around eighteen years of age, her perfectly toned body, fair skin, and attractive features made her the most expensive entertainer in the brothel. Nanda Masi adored her. After all, she brought in many customers.

"No, I don't! And why should I? Who gave me that name—Gauri? My parents, who left me to perish in this never-ending darkness. For what? For just … just five thousand rupees? I was barely twelve … They left me here to be raped … every day, every night. To be abused, hurt, kicked. I … I …" she was sobbing. I put a hand on her shoulder, which she shoved away roughly.

"Please. I don't need your sympathy. I am proud to have shed Gauri and emerge as Rosy. At least, my tormentors here, the customers … they are not people I trust. I expect nothing from them. I believe they are better humans than the two spineless creatures who gave birth to me." Her outburst was over, she plodded away clumsily, without looking at me. After closing the door behind her, I am sure she must have cried into the pillow on her creaky bed, with no hand to stroke her hair.

I heaved a sigh and went inside.

These dolled-up faces had stories to tell, memories to cherish or abandon. The dark dingy lanes were storehouses of heart-wrenching tales like Rosy's. I felt claustrophobic and restless. A sentence Ma used to say echoed in my head: "God never abandons his children. Be righteous, and he will do what's best for you!"

I believed her blindly, but would that mean I had not been righteous enough? Why else would I have landed in this infernal? Is it a sin to trust someone? My thoughts only brought me pain. Not all of my past was beautiful and worth remembering. Once upon a time, I had trusted someone.

CHAPTER 3

"Hey, do you remember Ramanuj?" Savita asked, a sly grin at the corner of her lips. She was my classmate, my neighbour, and also my bestie.

Every evening, Savita and I would visit the nearby garden and talk out hearts out. The topics ranged from school issues to problems at home. There was nothing under the sky we wouldn't confer about. We never kept secrets from each other. But that evening, I had lied to her.

"No," I replied, pretending to be thinking hard. "Ramanuj? Um … No, not at all!"

"Really?" she asked, disbelief evident in her voice. "The guy who came with my brother on my birthday? I thought you two had even talked!"

"Um. Maybe. I can't recall. Anyway, why are you asking me about him?"

"Well, my brother was telling me that Ramanuj likes you!"

"Likes me?" I frowned. "Well … so?"

"Come on, Era … you are not a kid!" She sounded irritated.

"I know I am not, but you know me, right? I am not interested in all this. Appa and Ma would be so mad. We are just fifteen, Savi!" I was trying my best to hide the excitement tickling my insides.

"Yeah. That's what! We are fifteen, and I already have a boyfriend! Why are you so boring, Era?"

"I don't know. Maybe I am just different!" I was trying to sound cool. "Anyway, I have to go. Ma asked me to return early today." I started to walk away saying, "Bye, Savi!"

"And what should I tell Ramanuj?" she yelled.

"N and O … No!" I shouted back as I ran home, even as I burst into an uncontrollable giggle.

Ma had not actually asked me to return early. But I wanted to. Just to be with myself and enjoy the moment.

＊ ＊ ＊

Of course, I remembered Ramanuj very clearly. In fact, he was the first face I had noticed on entering Savi's living room on her birthday evening. He was sitting on the couch, engrossed in his mobile phone. In a black T-shirt and blue denim, he reminded me of the male protagonist of a television soap Ma was addicted to. Though he was sitting, he looked tall. Fair complexion, black messy hair, and chocolate-boy features—he stood apart in the not-so-good-looking crowd.

"He is Ramanuj," Savi's brother whispered into my ears when he noticed me staring at his friend. Though I was embarrassed, I pretended otherwise. Later that evening, when Savi and I were sitting together, discussing the unfair attitude of some of our teachers, he approached us. Savi's brother tagged along.

"Hi," he said with twinkling eyes, wide grin and extended arm towards me "Ramanuj".

"Erawati," I replied with a shy smile, avoiding the handshake. At this, he awkwardly withdrew his hand and looked around to check if anybody was watching us. There was an uncomfortable and formal exchange of words before we bid adieu.

＊ ＊ ＊

Ramanuj's good looks and infectious boyish charm had left me feeling hypersensitive that night. But never, even in my wildest dreams, did I expect him, to show interest in me. After all, I was quite a plain Jane compared to his movie-star looks. Although my mother believed that I was the epitome of Indian beauty and personage, I was sure that her thoughts were heavily influenced by motherly instincts. She said my features were arresting and rare, a combination of the earthy sculpted south Indian beauty and soft, attractive eastern grace.

After returning home that evening, I headed straight to my room, my space of solace. The heady feeling of ecstasy forced me to hide my face in the pillow. I let my thoughts wander.

"Maybe Ma is right. Why else would he like me?" I thought aloud. It was a proud moment of self-content. "I like you too, Ramanuj," I had whispered softly to myself.

A sudden knock at the door brought my wandering thoughts back to reality. "Chameli, what are you doing inside? Open the door!" It was Nilofer. I opened the door and welcomed her with a poker face, into the darkness of my room and my thoughts.

"What has happened to you? You look awful!" she remarked, still staring at me in shock.

"Oh! No, nothing. Come inside," I answered, my thoughts partially hanging in the memory lanes of my past.

We both walked up to my bed and sat there. Neither of us spoke for a few seconds, and then it was Nilofer who broke the monotony of the unnerving silence that pervaded the room.

"Do you think you can sustain like this? Did you have breakfast?" she asked with genuine concern.

"No …" I looked at the floor, feeling guilty.

"Chameli, I am aware of your desire to go back to being Era again, but I do not want you to entertain false hopes. You should know that you cannot be Era again. This infernal has a way in but no way out. It will be a grotesque luxury to believe that our parents will rescue us. The reality is that normal people cannot even sneak into this world of darkness. This penurious territory is guarded by criminals and even part of the government …" Tears rolled down her dewy eyes as she spoke. "But we have to survive," she continued. "However ill we feel of our existences, we cannot end the lives God has given us. The unfeeling hypocritical society might shun us and look down upon us, but we have to stay strong. So, my friend, it is important for us to have proper food, sleep and maintain hygiene, so that we do not fall prey to the diseases that are a part and parcel of this life. As your well-wisher, I can just guide you. But at the end of the day, it is up to you. What you want to do with your life …?" Nilofer looked at me expectantly.

"Why don't you call me Era?" I asked, out of context.

"What?" she was definitely not expecting that question after all that she had said.

"Why don't you call me Era?" I repeated.

"Because you are not Era. You are Chameli, a sex worker. A daughter of the darkness. Era was a bright and beautiful child. Do you really feel you are still Era? Don't you think Chameli killed her the day she stepped into this place? What? Why are you quiet?" Nilofer was ruthless, determined to cut off Era from Chameli, determined to hold a mirror to my face.

"No! I am Era … Erawati Suresh Iyer … Era!" I was crying, hurt and defeated by reality. Yet, conviction resonated from the remains of my shredded self-esteem.

Nilofer embraced me with love and whispered softly, "I know the blows of indignity can hurt our exteriors, but internally you are Era and I am … I am Shahin. But acceptance of our fate will help us drink this poison better …"

Freeing myself from her embrace, I looked at her in surprise. "You never told me ..."

"My real name? Chameli, I didn't tell you because I didn't want to be reminded. I didn't want to be bombarded with memories that weaken me, thoughts that paralyze me. What's the point in mourning our fates and reminding ourselves that life could have been better? Nilofer is a prostitute, and she can never be Shahin again. I don't want to live in a fool's paradise, Chameli."

"But why? Ma used to say that God never abandons the righteous. Then why can't we dream of something better, something more meaningful?" I asked in a quivering voice.

"And didn't she tell you that Allah tests his favourite children? He is probably testing us too," she replied but with little conviction.

"But—"

"There is no but, Chameli, for God's sake!" Nilofer threw her hands in the air in desperation. "Accept your reality, please." When her anguish had passed, she looked at me with a mellowed expression. "Let's go and make breakfast. Come on. I was waiting for you, I am hungry. And Nanda Masi is not here today. Police have taken her for interrogation about a trafficking case. So, at least today, you are Era and I am Shahin."

I followed her, unsure of what to make of her words.

✶ ✶ ✶

The brothel of Kamathipura was a melting pot of diversities; it was even segmented based on the customers the girls could attract. Virgins were the costliest items in Nanda Masi's flesh market, and if they were beautiful, they were given the best treatment in terms of food and hygiene. Elite and wealthy customers were allowed to those rooms, and sex was prohibited without condoms.

Then there were us, the pretty non-virgins. We, too, were given enough food, and customers were instructed to use condoms. After all Nanda Masi and the other 'madams', as they were referred to in the brothels, would never want to lose their gold-egg-laying geese to AIDS or other dreadful sexually transmitted diseases. But there were girls in the brothel who were not as fortunate and were subjected to inhumane and unhygienic living conditions. They were mostly older women who had been in this business for long, or perhaps came from poor homes. Truck drivers, goons, and drunkards exploited them, for mere hundred or two hundred rupees. They didn't have clean beds, not even enough food. But to make them look voluptuous, they were given inexpensive drugs that made them susceptible to many diseases.

And finally, there were those who were caged like animals, let out only to eat or cater to a customer. The caged rooms were prohibited areas, where no one was allowed. Even we had only heard about them and never had the nightmarish experience of seeing those distressed souls trapped in hellish torture.

Life in the brothel was a struggle every moment. Crimes like child abuse, human trafficking formed the backbone of the flesh industry. Underworld mafia and many other antisocial elements, along with the police, reaped the fruits of the plants that were forced to flourish on the grounds of painful shrieks and mournful nights. Drugs and illegal alcohol trading were common in the area. The dark, dingy lanes of Kamathipura, like many other red-light districts, had many untold stories and agonies attached to it.

There were norms too. When it came to food, the girls generally prepared breakfast and lunch for themselves and also for their madams. Dinner, however, consisted of unhealthy food, ordered by the customers from nearby restaurants. On lucky nights, a wealthy customer could take the girls to starry hotels, if the sultry lanes didn't suit his class.

* * *

Dal was boiling; I was sitting in front of it and recollecting the conversation I had had with Nilofer, while she was busy making chapatis. We had planned to prepare dal and chapati for breakfast, and rice and some chicken for lunch.

"Chameli, is the dal ready? I am very hungry!"

"Hmm? Yeah, yeah, almost!"

Though Nanda Masi was not there, her shadow, Queen, was keeping an eye on us. We had enough food, but wastage was a punishable offence. She ensured that the girls abided by the norms of the brothel.

"Why are the two of you late for breakfast?" she inquired authoritatively.

"Um, actually, Chameli was not feeling well!" Nilofer replied.

"Hmm." She eyed me suspiciously for a moment. My downtrodden appearance probably convinced her. Granting me a miserly smile, she turned to Nilofer. "Make one chapati for me too." It was an order, not a request.

"Sure!" Nilofer replied with a generous smile. Her chapatis were famous for being soft and delicious, and Queen couldn't resist the temptation of having one.

About half an hour later, the three of us were seated on the floor in my room. We didn't want to eat in the dirty kitchen area, where most girls had their meals. Queen was reluctant to come with us, but eventually she agreed. As we sat eating, my mind was flooded with many questions. I never liked Queen, but after the gut-wrenching revelation of Rosy's sad past, I dared not nurture any preconceived notions. I wanted to know her, before attempting to judge from the way she conducted herself.

"What is your real name?" I asked.

Queen, who was enjoying her meal, was taken by surprise. "What?"

"I mean, I am Erawati. Nilofer is Shahin. What is your name?"

"Hmm. My story is different. I am Queen; that is my real and only name."

"You mean your parents named you Queen?"

"Why? Is it that bad?"

I didn't know what to say, so I kept quiet.

Queen giggled and continued, "Well a mother can name her daughter Queen, if she knows that the child will grow up to be a sex worker!"

Nilofer and I looked at each other and then at her, dazed. We had stopped eating to listen to her.

"Why are you looking at me like that? Huh? My mother was a prostitute in these brothels of Kamathipura. The queen bee of her time! And that's why my name is Queen. She died last year, at thirty-two. Um, of AIDS."

Her casual tone was unnerving. Nilofer and I gazed at each other, and then I made the unceremonious blunder of asking her, "And your father?" I immediately realized my mistake.

But it was too late, and the damage was already done.

"What?" she looked at me with disdain and disbelief. "Are you trying to insult me? If you conceive today, would you know who the father is? Born to 'so-called' good families … I don't know what you people think of yourselves! How dare you ask such questions?"

"No, I never meant to insult you. I am sorry!" I really was. After all, it was not her fault that she was born in a brothel, to an unknown father.

"Well, okay." Queen smiled, as if her fury was a joke.

We smiled too, unsure of how to react.

"Everyone is not lucky to have memories to hang on to, Era. Um, I mean, Chameli." Queen looked at me derisively. "I have always lived here; this is my home. I have never been to school. I have grown up watching my mother closing the door of our room with a new stranger, every night. Then gradually I realized that I was the daughter of a sex worker—an outcast. Huh! Who cares! I am happy, and I am not ashamed of my existence. You know last year, when my mother died, she made me promise that I will never leave these lanes. She said that the outside world was uglier." Queen stopped to look at us, and then continued, "I know most of the girls hate Nanda Masi. It's true she is harsh, but I love her. Because I am indebted to her." She paused as we gasped. "Surprised?" she asked with an eerie tinge of amusement in her eyes.

"Hmm." Nilofer nodded in affirmation.

Queen heaved a heavy sigh; the amusement had evaporated. "My mother was barely twelve and already married to a man triple her age. It was a remote village in Bihar, and needless to say, it wasn't uncommon to see young girls married away to men older than their fathers. My mother had accepted her fate. Tortured, assaulted … she was leading a dreadful life. There wasn't anything that she could do about it, except crying into her pillow in the silence of the dark lonely nights." She paused to breathe and also to procure the strength to narrate the agonies that she had held within herself for long. "But her fate held more stings in store. Her husband—an abusive, illiterate, alcoholic—died consuming poisonous liquor, and the entire village turned against her. Dipped in superstitions and conjectures, the unlettered society condemned her for bringing ill-fate to the family. She was barely a child, yet she was beaten up, starved, cursed, and tormented until the panchayat declared her a witch and decided to stone her to death." Queen had tears of hatred and anguish in her eyes.

We were speechless. The rumblings of such incidents do reach the literate ears of the educated society, but very feebly. Hence, Queen's tale of ignorance and hostility was heart-breaking for both of us.

"Petrified, my mother was waiting to die in immeasurable pain," Queen continued. "Anyway, Nanda Masi belonged to the same village. And when this ruckus of inhumanity was hovering above my mother's fate, fortunately, she was there. She had gone to the village to attend her mother's last rituals, discernibly against the wishes of her family. And when things were getting out of hand, she decided to leave. A day before she was to leave, she heard of my mother. And I have no idea how, but Nanda Masi managed to emancipate her from the fetters of cruelty and brought her here. This infernal was Elysium to my mother, and I feel the same. I had started to work when I was thirteen, and now, I am sixteen. Three years have passed. Yes! I sell my body … so what? I don't beg, borrow, or steal. I don't kill people. I sell what is my own, so what is wrong in what I do?"

I had no answer to her question, so I just looked on.

"You are not wrong," Nilofer said, gauging my inability to speak.

Happy with Nilofer's affiliation, Queen resumed eating as she spoke again, "You know, sometimes I feel I am luckier than both of you."

Her voice sounded lighter now; I don't know how she switched over that swiftly. But her words now were mixed with her munching, and what she said sounded like a raunchy cacophony. Presumably, her profession made it so that whatever she did or said had a forceful sassiness.

"See, I have experienced nothing but the sultry lanes of Kamathipura. So to me, this is the world. And I have no loss to mourn. I nurse no grievance of wrongs bestowed upon me, because I have lived no rights. Hahaha!"

Her laughter turned hysterical—hollow, spine-chilling. Nilofer and I exchanged uncomfortable glances.

"Anyway, thanks for the food," Queen said, and abruptly she got up to leave.

Nilofer and I looked at each other perplexed, for we weren't expecting such an unanticipated end to our discussion. We were dumbfounded by her revelations. Unarmed and clueless, we just watched her walk away with the plate in her hand.

Suddenly, she stopped mid-way. "Oh, Chameli …" she said, as if she was about to say something urgent to me. "Um, just a heads-up. You probably know that Nanda Masi isn't really pleased with your attitude. But things are getting worse. I suggest you start taking work more seriously and try to get into her good books. You see, um, there are rumours floating in the brothel that she might just put you in those caged rooms if you continue to throw your weight around. I hope you know what that means. I am not supposed to discuss this with you Chameli, but … but I thought that I should warn you. After all, everyone deserves a fair chance." Then, Queen walked away without waiting for my response.

Shaken by the revelation, I turned to Nilofer in panic.

I knew Nanda Masi didn't like me, but even in my wildest dreams, I couldn't have guessed this. "Take my work seriously how? Objectification of my existence isn't work to me. I am not a part of this brothel!" Some disturbing thoughts wreaked havoc in my mind, and I shut my ears with both hands. Tears of rancour wetted my cheeks. Nilofer walked up to me and wrapped me up in her warm embrace.

"Just accept your present. I know it is difficult, but just to avoid worse things … do it. Chameli needs to forget Era."

I knew she was right. "I … I will have to."

CHAPTER 4

After some time, Nilofer went to her room to get some rest, and solitude brought the insecurities back to me. The creaky fan was going round and round, incessantly. I lay on the bed and looked at it expectantly, but its endeavours couldn't evaporate the sweat drops on my forehead. Tears were wetting my dirty pillow; there I had no will to restrict them. They flowed down freely, with the remains of the kohl from last night's eye make-up, while I stared at the ceiling fan, oblivious of my surroundings.

My heart was thumping mercilessly, and it was difficult to breathe. Asphyxiated and terrified, I unknowingly started unwinding the knots inside my heart. I seldom attempted to loosen them, as they bled profusely, tearing my heart to pieces. But that day, the knots had voluntarily agreed to unwind. The ceiling fan made a creaky noise and an insufferable stink harassed me.

But soon, everything faded.

✳ ✳ ✳

I could hear the chirping of autumn birds and the suave movement of the flowing river in front of us. The sun was mellow and lulling. The soft grass would generally feel heavenly, but that dusk was different. I sat without an iota of ease, with my newfound femininity.

The area was famous for attracting young couples in search of a place where they were left alone with their hearts beating as one. Well, that is what I thought at that time, but later I knew what the riverside meant to them. It was a place where they could kiss and explore each other's body, stealthily, without getting noticed by the so-called moral policing brigade.

Ramanuj sat with equal uneasiness at a distance and barely looked at me. That was the first time I had successfully fought my conscience and responded to his plea of meeting in secret. He was a very attractive guy. Every fibre in my body pleaded with me to let him touch me. Even more so because my dearest friend Savita had fuelled the spark of love within me. But the thought of lying to Ma and Appa always left me sweaty with guilt. But this is the truth about lying: once you start being dishonest, your conscience gradually withers, and you are at ease with deceit.

Time passed as both of us stared at the river—aimless, shy and apprehensive. Ramanuj made the first move to break the ice. He rose to his feet and moved in my direction. My heart almost jumped to my mouth, and I awkwardly looked away. Then he sat by my side and looked at me intently for a few seconds, which felt like hours to me.

And then, finally, he spoke, "Are you comfortable, Era? I mean, you don't look … I … I am extremely sorry for forcing you into this. I never knew you would be so … so uneasy. I—"

"No," I interrupted him. "I mean, that's okay. Well, Savi told me that you wanted to meet me. She said you apparently wanted to say … say something. Please go ahead."

"Ahem!" he cleared his throat, as if he was about to start singing. An inaudible and invisible giggle was threatening to escape my throat, but I controlled it to save the moment.

"Yeah … I … I …" he fumbled pathetically, almost stirring sympathy in me.

"What?" I asked again, with as much grace and sweetness as I could afford.

"I like you, Era." Abruptly, he looked away.

I looked at him, dazzled, at this already-known fact being thrown at me so suddenly. In the eerie silence, we shared a few moments of sheer awkwardness. Feelings of guilt and happiness took over like a flash flood.

And then he spoke again. "Do you like me?"

I could not answer, but my eyes did. They must have sent some positive signals to him, which gave him the courage to hug me. It was a feeling I would cherish forever, no matter what life made of our relationship, of me and of him. My first real encounter with love would remain etched forever in my mind and body. He was warm, fragrant, and masculine.

"I know what you want to say," he whispered in my ears. I could feel his breath. "I know words are entangled in shyness, but I have heard those unspoken magical ones you want to convey. Thank you, Era. Thanks, my angel."

I had never felt as important as I did in that moment. Yet, I withdrew when he approached to kiss me on my lips. "No, Ramanuj. Please, not now." I mumbled.

"Okay, Era. I won't do it if you're not comfortable." He affectionately planted a peck on my forehead instead.

That evening was the beginning of a new era. An era that had gradually and stealthily crept into my life, and unknowingly made Ramanuj the centre of my living. Whatever I did or thought had something to do with him. I was as if trapped in an enjoyable turmoil of confusing emotions. It was like a cyclone. I could clearly see my parents contouring around me, while Ramanuj remained the eye of the storm. He beckoned my entangled feelings towards him like a magnet.

My books, pens, calculators—everything was afloat in the baffling movement of wind around me. I could see my parents look visibly disappointed at my decreasing marks in every passing exam. I wanted to yell at myself, "Get a hold of yourself Era! Look how you are tarnishing your Ma and Appa's faith in you. Slap yourself hard, break this spell … break this spell!" But no, the spell refused to let go.

* * *

"Era," I heard my mother call lovingly. "Get up, my dear, it's nine already. Don't you get up to see your favourite sunrise these days?"

I got up with a jolt and looked around. It was a Saturday morning, and I had been talking to Ramanuj till late into the night on the mobile phone he had gifted me. I was carefully exploring the surroundings to make sure that I had not left my phone anywhere in the visible range.

"What happened, Era? What are you looking for?"

"No, nothing!" I replied with a forced smile.

"Hmm. Era, I wanted to talk to you about something."

My heart leapt to my mouth. Her expression had also changed. A million questions started bulldozing through my brain. "Is it anything to do with Ramanuj? Have Ma and Appa spotted us together? Or maybe someone in the society or school complained about us?"

"Era! Are you listening to me?" Ma demanded. There was anguish, hurt, and disappointment mixed in her voice. The feelings were difficult to dissect.

"Yes, Ma!" I replied, trying to stop my voice from trembling or cracking.

"Era, in the last six months or so, I and your Appa have seen a drastic change in your attitude. You always keep to yourself. Your studies have suffered too. My Era was never an average student. She was a star performer. Who is this child sitting in front of me? Yes, she looks like Era but doesn't behave like her. What is wrong, tell me?"

I could see teardrops at the corner of her eyes. Fangs of guilt spread poison into my heart. I was sitting unarmed in front of a woman I had always revered. I had never felt so helpless in my life.

"Era, tell your Ma. Why does the rising sun not invite your imaginations anymore? Why don't you sit with your Appa and watch National Geography and Discovery in the evening these days? Why are your grades deteriorating? And why … why did your maths teacher, who once thought you were her pride, call us to meet her yesterday?" Her voice cracked midway.

"Sangeeta Ma'am called you?" The sky broke on my head. I pleaded with God to reduce me to ashes.

"Yes, she did. Appa and I went to meet her yesterday. Era, who is Ramanuj?" she enquired looking straight into my eyes. I looked away to avoid that penetrating, questioning glare.

"Ma … Ma …" I fumbled.

"Go on. Erawati."

"A friend!" I blurted out.

"A friend?" she frowned. "A really good friend he must be. Otherwise, why would you spend all your spare time in school with him?" Her sarcasm hurt. "And I don't remember you missing school of late. Then why is your attendance poor, Era?"

I had no reply. I looked down and hot tears of humiliation rolled down my cheeks.

Ma was exasperated. I could make out she was dealing with her anger, and it took her a good few seconds to calm herself down. "Era, we all have been through your age, and believe me, it's perfectly normal to feel the way you are feeling for that boy. No, you are not a criminal. You are just experiencing adolescence."

She drew closer to me. But I could barely look up.

"Era, just remember one thing. Having feelings for someone isn't wrong, but cheating yourself, your studies, your parents … that is

wrong my child. At your age, it is tough to make out the difference between wrong and right. It all looks rosy and beautiful. But the reality is not always so. You are a bright child; don't lose yourself to external needs and abandon your virtues. Promise me, Era, that you will study hard and regain your lost position. Promise me ..." She held her hand out to me, which I reciprocated with an unsure touch of my trembling right hand. "I don't know Ramanuj," she continued. "Maybe he is a good boy and as bright as you are. But you guys are too young. This is the time for you to build your future." She paused to look at me. "Okay, cheer up! Now that you have promised to give me my Era back, I will prepare your favourite breakfast. Come on now, get up. Take a bath and come for breakfast, princess. Your old Appa and Ma will be waiting."

I embraced her with all my might "Ma, I am sorry. I will never let you down. Never, I promise!"

That morning, I vowed to myself that my love for Ramanuj would never weigh heavy on the faith that my parents have in me.

✳ ✳ ✳

Later that day, I was sitting in solitude, but his thoughts wouldn't leave me alone. I kept thinking of him and in that superfluity of emotions, I realized that in the last six months of knowing him, I had actually learnt nothing about him or his family. He was amongst the hundreds of rich kids who came to Coonoor for good educational facilities. Our little hamlet held many prestigious institutions in its charming abode of nature, which attracted students from all parts of India and also abroad. But beyond this information, I knew little about his family dynamics.

Practically, I wasn't from a background that could afford such expensive schools. However, Appa had dreams—really big ones. He had not only stretched his financial limits for my schooling but also made sure that I never felt deprived or belittled. He even got me a laptop, so that I would not be left behind the rest of my classmates.

But things were very different for Ramanuj. His parents were famous doctors. His mother practised psychiatry in Dubai and father was a heart surgeon based in London. So finance was the last item in their worry list. However, Ramanuj seldom discussed his family. In fact, I had sensed a strange uneasiness in his body language whenever I mentioned them.

✻ ✻ ✻

On Monday, I reached school with conflicted emotions. I had not spoken to Ramanuj after Friday night, and I knew he would be anxious and annoyed. I entered my classroom with a poker face, with no clue of how to face the situation. I was barely able to concentrate. As lunch break approached, the thumping rhythm of my heart jumped from one scale to the one above. And at last, it was time to face him.

He was standing at the edge of the corridor, overlooking the school ground. His eyes were fixed on the children playing football. His look was intense. I stealthily approached him from behind and lovingly placed my hand on his right shoulder. He immediately turned around. Dark, questioning eyes, hiding a mellowed fire, looked straight at me. Momentarily, I was shaken, but I collected my fragmented self and mustered my courage to face Ramanuj.

"Hi," I said, with a forced smile.

"Hello, Era," he replied and turned away.

"I know you must be angry, but I want to explain things to you. I am sure you will understand." The vulnerability was palpable in my voice, which must have quenched his fired ego to some extent. His eyes began to soften.

"Whatever it is Era, you could have just left me a text message

or answered just one … just one of my numerous calls! Keeping someone as anxious as I was, is not what I expect from you, Era." His accusatory tone made me feel almost like a criminal.

"I am sorry, very sorry! But there is something that I want you to know. Um …" I looked down and wracked my brain for the appropriate words. "Sangeeta Ma'am informed my parents about you and me. They had come to meet her. And on Saturday morning, Ma confronted me with these latest developments …"

"What? Did she hit you or scold you? What happened, Era?" He sounded anxious and scared.

"Ramanuj, my Ma is not like that. My parents did not hit me or scold me. In fact, Ma sympathized with my adolescent feelings and assured me that she understood. But at the same time, she urged me to set my priorities right. I—"

Ramanuj cut me short. "And what you mean by that? To strike me off your priority list, huh?"

"No, Ramanuj. I just want some time, not just for myself but for you too. We are too young, too vulnerable, our priorities at this stage should be academics and not romance. I want you to understa—"

"Wait, wait, wait, Erawati! This is not you!" He rolled his eyes and threw up his arms in a strange, scary manner. "This is your mother … she is speaking for you!" Before he could say something else, the bell rang, marking the end of the lunch break.

The bell was ringing and ringing, never to stop. I put both my hands on my ears and tried to muffle the pounding sound.

CHAPTER 5

Drenched in perspiration, I woke up—back in reality, in the lanes of Kamathipura. Unable to bear the silence of my surroundings, I walked over to Nilofer's room next door. She opened immediately after the first knock and welcomed me with a smile.

"Feeling better now? We will have lunch in a while. I will make for both of us, okay?" she delivered with assurance.

"Hmm," I replied absentmindedly. "Nilofer?"

"What?"

"Have you accepted yourself?"

"Well, maybe or maybe not. Honestly, I don't know. But I have realized that I do not have the heart to attempt fleeing from this dreadful trap, so whatever good or bad I do with my life, I have to do it here, right in the heart of this infamous red-light area. I hope I am able to nurture that lotus in the muddy waters of Kamathipura." She paused to breathe, as if the air would carry conviction into her lungs. "You may think I am being stupid, and probably I am, but I don't have any other means to keep myself alive. This hope of doing something worthwhile in the darkness of these lanes keeps me going."

"Can't we run away? Police, any NGO ... can nobody help us?"

"Shh! The walls have ears in this brothel."

"But—" I started, only to be stopped again.

"It is not that I have never considered that. But a few months before you came here, I witnessed something that has broken my backbone and ..." She paused, drops of sweat appearing on her forehead.

"What had happened?"

"Have you noticed that small room at the extreme right-hand corner of the corridor?" she asked in a low voice.

I nodded in response.

"They call it the torture room. It was about two months before you came here. They had brought a girl called Lilac, probably trafficked from Goa. Around fifteen years old, she was said to be breathtakingly beautiful. Nanda Masi was invigorated with Lilac's arrival, hoping to bring in high-end customers. But soon, she understood that the girl was not a crack-able nut at all. After numerous failed attempts of taming her, Nanda Masi finally labelled her as a rebel and discarded her as a useless addition to the brothel. And that marked the beginning of a dark period for that young life." Nilofer stopped and closed her eyes in disapproval of what was done to Lilac.

"What happened to Lilac?" I clung to her hands.

"I don't know the entire thing. No one does. There was so much hush-hush about the whole incident that all we got to know was that she was thrown to the pimps, like a piece of meat is thrown to hungry dogs. I … I can't even imagine the kind of torture she went through. Deprived of food, medical help … some say she died, and some say she was murdered." Nilofer had tears of anguish gushing out of her eyes. Her frail body shivered slightly, and her fair cheeks turned pink.

"Did you ever see her, Nilofer?"

Wiping off the tears, she answered, her voice anxious, "Hmm, just once. By then she had grown frail and sick. That day the door of the torture room was open, and I saw her sitting cross-legged on the bed, her head hung low. Even from a distance, I could clearly see bloodstains on the bedsheet. "And just as I was looking at her, an inebriated tormentor walked into the room and closed the door behind him. After that, there was silence; the muffed, traumatized groans couldn't reach my ears. But before the door was shut, she had looked up, and for a fraction of a second, her eyes had met mine. That gaze had penetrated my soul. I could see the fire in her eyes, which had not died, though her body gave away ..." Tears wetted Nilofer's cheeks, her voice quivered, yet she continued, "But Chameli. I am not Lilac. I won't be able to bear that magnitude of pain. I am weak ... very weak." She was now weeping. "I have not accepted myself, but I am not Lilac. I am too weak to protest!"

I moved a bit closer to her and held her tight. "You are not weak. We are not weak!" I assured her. "I will make lunch for you; you take rest."

As I was climbing down the stairs towards the kitchen, the image of a helpless young girl, caged like an animal in that torture room, floated in my mind.

I returned an hour later, with chicken curry and rice for lunch. We sat on the floor of Nilofer's room and ate silently. Clearly, Lilac and the fate she was subjected to had impacted Nilofer's convictions to the core. Though she appeared mature and sorted, inside, she was just a teenager, scared of her surroundings and the adversities her life was subjected to.

"Are you okay?" I asked, and for a moment, felt amused with the role reversal.

"Yeah, I think so." She smiled back.

"Why didn't you tell me about Lilac before?"

"I didn't want to scare you."

"But I am not scared."

"You might have been, if you had seen those eyes. A pair of bloodshot eyes haunted me for months. I could not sleep. They asked why I was so silent, so scared."

I hugged Nilofer, and she wept in my arms. And I kept thinking, "Is it really possible to find meaning in this life, in this dungeon?"

CHAPTER 6

It was a silent afternoon in the brothel. Nanda Masi was in police custody since morning. This wasn't new for her. She was a veteran in the flesh trade, drug market, and human trafficking. She was seasoned in facing police interrogations. In fact, she had mastered the art of escaping the dire aftermaths of her deeds. In her absence, the place seemed to me like a hostel without its warden. The girls heaved some sighs of relief and behaved more like their original selves, their actual age.

I was standing in the corridor that overlooked the lane where the girls displayed themselves to potential customers. Sunlight seldom made its way to that part of the city. A bewildering crisscross of dilapidated, crestfallen structures prevented the rays of hope from touching that godforsaken land. I gazed at the unseen woebegone spirit of the place. Some girls had already taken their positions and were passing lewd signals to the men who visited the area for their share of paid ecstasy. Soon, Nilofer joined me.

The place was a trap. Young girls would be sold like commodity, to the ladies who owned the rooms. Then they would be caged and asked to pay the money that was spent to buy them. With time, that amount would double, triple, and quadruple—leaving the girls with no choice but to sell themselves. The interest rates here were based on calculations that no actual mathematician can endorse. This brothel was quicksand, pulling us all deeper and deeper, until we could no longer endure sunlight and shied away from it willingly.

"No business today?" asked Nilofer.

"Not well. Besides, I have already paid this month's rent and instalment. I'll take the day off."

"But won't Nanda Masi scold you for that?"

"I told her in the morning that I was feeling sick. It's fine. From tomorrow, I won't take any risk. I will work regularly."

"Hmm, actually, I have similar plans." Nilofer winked.

"Oh! That's great!"

"Yeah!"

"Nilofer, can I ask you something?"

"What?" She sounded terse, as if she had already guessed my question.

"No, I mean … we talk so much, we are friends, but …" I faltered.

"What do you want to ask, Chameli? How I landed here, in this hell? That is what you want to know, right?"

"Nilofer, I am sorry. I don't mean to pry. I was just … I … I am sorry!" I fumbled pathetically.

She immediately mellowed down, perhaps feeling bad for the harshness in her tone. "No, no it's okay. I am sorry."

She sat down on the floor, as if something heavy had been suddenly placed on her head and the weight was forcing her to sit down. I followed suit.

"It was around a year back. I was brought here and sold to Nanda Masi just about three months before you came. I am from the slums of Mumbai. My father is a worker in a leather bag store in Dharavi. We are 6 sisters, and I am the eldest. It was not an easy life, Chameli. Poverty and hunger were perpetual parts of our lives." She paused, perhaps recalling her life as a teenager in the slums. "But my Abbu was an eternal optimist and whatever be the circumstance, he vowed to send us to school. I was performing well in academics, and he and Ammi would never stop bragging about my marks to our friends and relatives. They started dreaming of a better life through my success. But all dreams don't come true, especially for poor people."

"You can stop if this hurts you," I said, overwhelmed.

"It does, but I don't want to stop." She smiled cheerlessly. "It is important to shed off the baggage before starting afresh. All this time, I kept my agonies to myself. And that sore spread more and more. Maybe sharing with a friend will help me recover."

"I believe so," I replied confidently

"Really? But you have never confided in anyone."

"I know, but I will. I will …"

"Hmm, you should. For your own solace and stability. Anyway, life in the slums was marked with many big and small straits, but we were happy in our small abode of imperfections. Despondency attacked our lives, when my youngest sister, who was hardly two years old then, was detected with leukaemia." At this, her voice faltered. She had to restart with visible effort. "We were very poor; her treatment wasn't an affordable affair for us. Hopelessness engulfed our household, and during that state of mental instability, my father's distant cousin extended a helping hand. He promised to help me get a job in the city. Initially, my parents were reluctant, but their stand weakened with the continuous deterioration of my sister's condition."

"What work, Nilofer?"

"Domestic help." She paused, and then started in a slightly different tone, "He said that they paid well, and I could also continue school. Strangely, his exaggerated enthusiasm never aroused any suspicion in us. Quite hypnotically, he convinced Ammi and Abbu to let me accompany him. He promised to get me enrolled in an agency that supplied domestic help to households." The pain of these memories was etched on Nilofer's face. "I remember it was a cloudy morning. The winds were strong and fiendish. Ammi wasn't feeling comfortable. There was an unsaid, unexplained lack of ease in her." By now, it was as if Nilofer was speaking to herself.

"'Don't send her with him,' pleaded Ammi. 'Fatima, you are being childish now. He will just enrol her name in that agency's list, so that when an opportunity comes, they can contact us,' assured Abbu. But Ammi was not convinced. 'So why does he need her to accompany him?' she asked. 'Shahin's Abbu … I am not comfortable with this cousin of yours. Why don't you go with them?' Fatima, we have known him for years.' But Ammi shot back, 'And don't you remember he had disappeared in the past and returned after months of exile? Only Allah knows where he was during that time, and what he did. How can you trust him so much?' Poor Abbu, he was in a fix! 'I would have gone with them,' he said, 'but you know that Maalik is opening a new store today. How can I take leave now, Fatima?' 'Allah! I am feeling so restless,' Ammi exclaimed. 'My heart is pounding. I can't go with them either; who will take care of Naazim in my absence?' Ammi collapsed on the floor, her hand on her head in desperation."

Nilofer paused and took a deep breath before carrying on.

"And then, I reassured Ammi. I said, 'Don't be so scared. I will be back in a few hours. Chachu said it's not too far.' But as it turned out, that was the last time I saw Ammi. Soon, Chachu came. He had a cab waiting outside. I got in and bid adieu to my life forever. I still remember Ammi and Abbu waving at me. Ammi was weeping, with Naazim in her lap …" Nilofer smiled wryly. "No one suspected anything, but Ammi could feel it. I am still awestruck by a mother's instinct."

"In the car, I asked Chachu how far we were from the agency?" 'Not much,' he told me. His tone had changed; he sounded harsh. I wanted to get back to my house desperately. 'Um, can we go some other day? I am not feeling well,' I said, without looking at his eyes. But Chachu did not reply. Instead, he ordered the cab driver to take the shorter route to Kamathipura. I froze. I had heard of that place. 'Kamathipura?' I asked in shock. 'Yes,' he said, 'Kamathipura. The agency is there. 'And suddenly, there was hollow laughter. The cab driver joined in too."

Nilofer closed her eyes, trying to hold back her emotions. Then, she resumed, "Tears of betrayal, insecurity, and fear welled up in my eyes. I immediately took out the mobile phone from my bag and started dialling Abbu's number. To my utter disbelief and panic, Chachu slapped me hard across my face and threw the phone out of the car. Anticipating my next move, he tied my hands with a rough rope and put a black tape on my lips. Then he pulled up the dark glasses of the windows. His eyes had attained a wolfish look by then. 'You think you are very smart? You think you can escape? You will never see your parents again. They won't be able to reach you. The place you are going to … it has doors that lead in but no doors to lead out!' He laughed like a mad man. Muffled, strangled moans and a never-ending flow of tears … that car ride was the beginning of it all. I remember that vicious laughter, Chameli. And I don't think I will ever forget it. That scary, hollow laughter still echoes within me on dark, lonely nights."

Nilofer turned to look at the girls in the lane. One of them was calling out to a guy who was watching her from a distance. There were others pulling up their skirts to expose their legs. We looked away. Strangely, yet fortunately, being there for almost a year had not altered our spirits. But that also meant going through incredible trauma each night.

Nilofer spoke up again. "When I was displayed to Nanda Masi, Chachu asked her, 'How is she?' This fat, hideously dressed woman, chewing beetle leaves—Nanda Masi—scanned me from head to toe and exclaimed, 'Beauty!' She smiled at me; I looked away. 'But very childish,' Nanda Masi said. Then, she commented on my apple-like complexion, pink lips, round black eyes. She called me a 'good catch'. All this while I could not comprehend whatever was happening to me. 'Ammi and Abbu must be waiting for me, they must be restless, Ammi must be weeping.' That's all I was thinking. But I had no means of reaching out to them. I felt like tearing myself into pieces. I wanted to kill that man I had called 'Chachu'."

The anger was evident on Nilofer's face. "That disgusting man, he was bargaining for me. 'Good things come at good prices. Nanda Masi,' he said with a wink.

At this, I lost myself, unable to hold back the rage. 'Chachu! You are selling me to this woman? I am like your daughter! Abbu won't spare you! Allah won't forgive you ever! You traitor!' Nanda Masi chuckled. 'My child, everyone shouts like this when they come here. Don't worry. It is not as bad as you think!' She winked at Chachu and approached me with open arms. I recoiled. 'Please don't touch me. My mother is crying at home; she will die if I don't return. Please, Aunty, please leave me,' I pleaded. But Nanda Masi replied sternly, 'She will learn to live without you.' I begged and begged. 'My sister is ill,' I said, 'we need money for her treatment. I will work but not here, never!' Nanda Masi's reply became crueller. 'You don't have a choice, my dear,' she said. 'I can tame wild cats, and you are not even wild. Just keep quiet, shh!' She put a finger on her lips and rolled her eyes in anger. Then she turned to Chachu and said, 'Your catch is already throwing a hell lot of tantrums. Not a penny more than 50,000.' 'What?' Chachu shouted. 'Masi, are you nuts? Only 50,000 for her? Anyone would give at least a lakh. Look at her!' I was dying inside as they went on bargaining over me. Finally, they settled on 70,000. That was my price."

Nilofer and I had been talking for more than an hour. She looked weak from all the crying. "Chameli, in front of my own eyes, I was sold like chattel. To this life of darkness, never to see light again. She named me Nilofer, and Shahin died. I thought about running away, but Lilac and many others slowly broke my confidence. Nanda Masi was right. I am not even wild. Only Allah knows how Ammi and Abbu are doing. Only Allah knows if my little sister survived." Nilofer closed her eyes once more, to deal with the turmoil in her heart.

CHAPTER 7

It's had been a day of revelations. I could hardly digest one story when another tragic tale came roaring towards me. It was also a day when I learnt to stop pitying myself. "Why me … why me … why me?" the question had no answer. And there was no point in trying to find one. There was no point in running after a mirage.

Nilofer was still by my side, sobbing and weak. I was holding her tight.

"Era," she called.

"What? *Now* why do you call me that?" I asked, partly amused, partly curious. "You have asked me to live in the present, right?"

"I have always wanted you to accept your present, because somewhere I felt that there was no way out. But, Era, I really do not know how to make this life meaningful. I lied to you. I have no idea in my drought-stricken brain that can transform us into Eos of this infernal. I am a weak girl who has lost everything … everything Era!"

I did not expect her to be my torchbearer in that dungeon, but this confession still hurt. "The school bell was loud and harsh, but even harsher was his look …" I mumbled.

"Whose?" Nilofer asked surprised.

"Ramanuj," I said as if I had uttered the obvious.

I was transported to the past.

✳ ✳ ✳

The school bell had rung sharp and loud that day. It's ringing echoed through my heart even days after. Ramanuj was also a changed person. His eyes were dry and emotionless. He neither smiled at me nor scowled. I had no idea what was going on in his head. All I knew was that my heart was bleeding. I wanted to break the awful silence that had intruded the space between our hearts. I was restless, helpless. I knew of no elixir that could heal it all. But patience cannot keep your emotions bound within the unseen boundaries of your heart for too long. So, at last, I took action. I sent him a message through a common friend and requested him to wait for me by the riverside after school.

When I reached the spot, the clouds were lying low. Ramanuj was looking at the silvery, swollen waters dispassionately, leaning on his bike. He looked striking, and my heart instantly started pounding rapidly. I approached him from behind and softly called his name, "Ramanuj?"

Immediately, he turned to look. He looked sick, with dark circles around his eyes, jawline tensed, and eyebrows knitted in a frown. I was taken aback for a few seconds, but I collected myself and smiled at him.

"Ramanuj …" I repeated and walked a few more steps closer to him.

"Hmm?" he asked. "If you do not want to carry on with our relationship, why do you need to meet me? Only to torment me more?"

"No, Ramanuj. I just wanted you to give ourselves some time. I never … I never said it's over." Internally, I cursed myself, "What have you done to him?"

Ramanuj gave me a shrug and a harsh smile "Don't you think I can understand what is going on—this fuss? You mother warned you to stay away from me, and you obliged. Time, education, establishment … all that is nonsense!"

"Ramanuj, it is not nonsense. Ma has promised me that she will

unite us if both of us study hard and establish ourselves and our love. Ramanuj … she never lies!"

"Really? And what are we supposed to do till then? Be 'friends' …?"

"I can understand your scepticism, but don't you too think that we need to prove ourselves before romancing through the days crucial in building our futures? You tell me Ramanuj!"

"No!" he shouted.

I was scared; I had never seen him like this. His eyes were fiery and lips dry. Tears forced their way down my face but went unnoticed.

"No," he repeated, softly this time.

Then there was just awkward silence, which seemed like hours. It had started to rain, and the riverside was spookily empty by then. The water level had also risen, but we did not even notice. In the dark shadow of the grey clouds, in the midst of a heavy downpour, we stood facing each other.

"What establishment are you talking about? No amount of money, no amount of success can buy you the happiness that true love can. Do you understand?" he shouted. "My parents are doctors. They are 'established' … and very much so! Filthy rich, successful … but have you ever heard me talking about them? Come on, Era, ask me why!"

"Why?" My lips were trembling, as was my body.

"Because they don't keep me with them. Because they stay separately in different parts of the world and continue to 'establish' themselves. Hahaha!"

His hollow laughter was killing me. I felt weak in the knees.

"And you and your mother talk about establishment to me … ME?" he shrieked.

"Ramanuj, let's leave. Please, I am scared … please," I pleaded.

"Scared, Era?" he rolled his eyes. "Why? Are you scared of the rain

or me? Tell me?"

"Ramanuj. Look at the river and the sky. Please, I beg of you, start the bike. Let's go!"

"No, Era. Why don't we jump into the river and kill ourselves? Then no one will ever be able to separate us." There was madness in his eyes.

"No!" I yelled in panic.

Ramanuj softened at the sight of my trembling. "Don't worry, I won't kill you. Come we will leave. My parents have abandoned me with riches, devoid of love. You have abandoned me to build your future. But I won't harm you, Era. Because I love you. I have spent most of my life with my grandparents or in luxurious hostels; family life is a distant dream for me. And it will continue to be so. My grandma and grandpa are the only people I am close to, and that will continue to be so, Era. Erawati, the dedicated daughter ... I will take you safe and sound to your Ma and Appa. Who cares even if I die after that!"

Tears of dejection fell from his eyes. I had noticed them, even though he looked away. "I care," I said. Indifferent to my surroundings, I approached him and hugged him tight. The lightning tightened my grip even more. We were completely drenched in the heavy downpour and in our emotions. Ramanuj did not reciprocate; he did not hug me back. But I continued to hold him till he was forced to respond.

I looked up at his eyes. My chin was touching his chest. Moments passed as we continued to look into each other's eyes. And then, he lowered his face and let his lips touch mine. I did not resist. The lightning in the sky was ineffectual when compared to the current that ravaged my insides. I was melting like wax; burning like a candle ... I just did not want that moment to pass.

We kissed for ages. Then I felt his hand pulling my shirt out, which I had tucked inside the skirt, and then his fingers started feeling my body. They moved up and down and up and down. Currents shot inside me, making me feel weak. A plethora of emotions brewed in my heart, and I closed my eyes.

When we reached the lane near my house, it was 8 p.m. He dropped me at a point not visible from the premises of my home. It was still drizzling. I slowly walked and looked back at Ramanuj several times, unsure of how to face my parents. They must have been so worried; I just hoped they did not inform the police. Savita knew of our meeting. "I hope she has not spilt the beans," I prayed.

Ma opened the door before I could press the calling bell. "Where were you?" she shouted in anger and relief. Appa, too, stood up from the couch. They were looking ghastly tensed. I felt like killing myself.

"I … I … Ma, I went to the riverside with a few friends. We got stuck; none of us had mobile phones. So …"

"Riverside? You went to the riverside in this weather? Who were you with, huh? Who was with you? Speak up, Erawati!"

"Nandini, let her in first," Appa said, without looking at me. "Erawati, go and change, or you will catch a cold."

I walked in, muddying up the floor of the living area. I didn't make eye contact. When I reached my room, I closed the door and almost immediately heard Ma speak.

"Suresh, I am sure she was with that boy. What has gone wrong with our child?"

"Nandini, hold yourself together. We will talk to her," assured Appa.

I did not go to the living area after changing my clothes. Instead, I sat on my bed, gazing at the rain through the window.

Sometime later, Ma and Appa came to my room. They sat down on the bed, by my side. After a few awkward moments of silence, Appa spoke, "Erawati, were you with the boy your mother is talking about?"

I did not answer, instead fiddled with my hair and stared at the bedsheet.

"Your father has asked you something, Era. We expect an answer!" Ma sounded angry. "You were with Ramanuj all this time, right? Savita is your best friend, and she returned directly from school. Who are these friends you went to the riverside with?"

I was silent.

"Era, don't be sacred. Tell us the truth," Appa urged.

"Yes," I muttered, almost inaudibly.

"What? Louder!" Appa ordered, with a tinge of anger in his voice.

"Yes, Appa," I replied again, a bit louder this time, with my eyes still fixed on the bedsheet.

"I warned you not to! You promised you will study hard and stop this lovey-dovey business, Era. Yet, you went with him again? I am ashamed of you!" Ma was yelling in a way I had never heard before.

I was shaken but did not cry or look up.

"Hmm." Appa had been silent through Ma's outburst. "Nandini let me talk to her, please."

"What, what will you tell her? Nobody matters to her anymore except that ... that Ramanuj!" She almost spat out his name in disgust. It hurt me, but I was silent.

"Nandini, I want to talk to her," he repeated, this time much more firmly. Ma was immediately quiet. After taking a deep breath, Appa turned to me. "Erawati, I won't ask you what you were doing with that boy, but I want to know something. What do you want from life? I don't want to burden your conscience with guilt, but I want you to know one thing. We are ordinary people, Era. Education is our one and only means of survival. Your friend, Ramanuj, must be from some rich family. His sensibilities; his thoughts may not be the

same as ours. It is for you to decide your priorities. Children at your age always go through this. You are not an exception. But getting you back to the right track is our duty. Era, you know that I and Nandini are believers of true love. But just like your mother had said, give yourselves time … time to outgrow immaturity so that you can differentiate between good and bad."

Tears were flowing down my cheeks.

"Era," he continued, "I know it is difficult, but we are with you through this rough patch of your life. Invite Ramanuj over, and I will explain to that kid as well. Don't think we hate him; he is just a young boy. He is behaving his age. I am sure his parents would advise him the same, if they came to know."

"No, they won't," I said to myself but audible enough for Appa to hear.

"What? Why do you say that?"

"Because his parents don't care about him. They are famous doctors placed in different parts of the world. He stays with his grandparents. He has rarely tasted the essence of togetherness of a family, Appa," I mumbled.

"Hmm!" he exclaimed.

"I feel guilty when I see him. I feel guilty when I see you and Ma. This guilt is killing me, Appa. I just don't know what to do." I was weeping by now.

"So now I know what is hurting you, my little angel. But there is a solution to every problem," Appa said lovingly, melting my heart. "Call him over for lunch this weekend. I want to meet this young chap, okay?"

I hugged him tight, though I was not too sure if Ma endorsed this arrangement. But she kept quiet.

The next morning, the first thing I did after reaching school was meet Ramanuj. And he was equally anxious to meet me.

"Hey, Era. What happened after you reached home yesterday?" he asked.

"As expected," I answered.

"Did they hit you? Scold you?"

"No, I told you, Ramanuj, they are different. Yeah, Ma was very upset, even Appa was. And of course they rebuked me for being out in that weather. But I have something to tell you."

"What?" He looked scared.

"No, no, don't be worried. They have invited you over for lunch, at our place, this Saturday." I smiled.

"Really? Wow! That's kind of unbelievable!"

"Didn't I tell you my Appa and Ma are not ordinary people? They think differently. And they don't even hate you!" I assured. "Okay, now tell me what do you like? Vegetarian or non-vegetarian? We have both. My Appa is a strict vegetarian, Tamil Brahmin, but my Ma is a fish-eating Bengali. You can choose whatever you want!"

"Well, given a choice, I am non-vegetarian," he said, finally smiling.

"Okay! Now I am going. Maths class is about to start, bye!"

"When are we going to the riverside again?" Ramanuj asked with a wink.

"Uh, don't be so optimistic! Let me see, maybe tomorrow or next week or next month. All depends on my mood, mister!"

"Really? And what can this humble servant do to uplift mademoiselle's mood?" he asked dramatically.

"Stop it! Just concentrate on your studies. This mademoiselle is happy only when you get great marks in exams, got it?"

"Hmm, got it! Meet you during lunch then. Bye!"

"Bye, Rama."

During lunch, we sat together. We were eating ravenously, when suddenly, Ramanuj asked, "Why are your parents keen to meet me?"

"Hmm? I don't know. Appa will probably ask you to concentrate on your studies now, and once we both are doing well, we could then think of dating each other ..."

"Then?"

"What then?"

"No, I mean, what are we supposed to do? I am confused, Era."

"Ramanuj, listen to me, relax. I have thought a lot. Everything is in our hands. If this relationship doesn't hamper our studies, or our reputation, my parents will never pose a threat to our love. They will happily unite us. It's just that for the time being, studies, career, and self-development should be our priorities before anything else."

"But Era, doesn't that mean ...?"

"No, it doesn't mean that we are breaking up. We will be together and always. Just one small request. Will you keep my request, Ramanuj?" I looked at him affectionately.

"Anything for you," he replied.

"Hmm. Physical intimacy should be limited at this stage. Don't think I regret anything that happened between us, but we are just too young, too vulnerable. Please, Rama."

"Okay, Era. I will never do anything against your will, you know that, right?"

"Of course. I love you, Ramanuj."

"I love you, Erawati."

CHAPTER 8

"**A**nd you never made love again Era?" Nilofer asked inquisitively.

My eyes were moist, but not with grief. "Haha. I will be honest. We did touch, many times, again and again … it is like that forbidden fruit! But it wasn't sex, just physical intimacy. I have never had sex with Ramanuj. Nilofer … um, do you mind if I call you Shahin, just for today?"

"No, not at all!" she replied with a smile.

The sun had mellowed and there was a crimson hue all around. The dingy lane was far more crowded. The flesh market was warming up for the evening. Customers with varied demands pottering around—some wanted fair, some wanted dark, some wanted fat, some wanted thin. Everything in the brothel was just skin-deep, nothing touched within.

Women with dolled-up faces and often broken hearts stood along the lane in sleazy postures passing sexual comments to potential customers. The place was like a pot-boiler movie. Each face had a different tale and so did each wandering man who came to the dark premises of the infamous red-light area.

"Look at them, Era. Many of them are like us—forced into prostitution."

"For sure. Shahin, this day has been eventful for me so far. I have learnt to read the pain behind that abhorrent make-up, and that there is life beyond the melancholy that shadows my heart. You know, I am not feeling as nauseated as I generally do." I took a deep breath.

"Good, Era. You know what? I love your name."

"Really?" I asked, surprised.

"E-r-a-w-a-t-i! Sounds like some princess's name—grand,

graceful! I love it, even the short form—Era. Like honey … a very sweet name. Does it have a meaning?"

"Yeah. it's the name of a river. It also has some Java origin. I don't know much about that." I shrugged. "And Shahin?"

"Shahin? It actually has many meanings. When used for a baby girl it means gentle or soft, but it also means a falcon," she replied.

"Hmm, so a falcon can also fall prey, huh?" Shahin nodded. "Anyway, aren't you feeling hungry, Shahin? We have been talking through the afternoon. I feel drained now," I confessed.

"Me too! Let's make some tea and have it with the biscuits I have in the cupboard!"

"Sounds great!"

With cups of tea and lots of biscuits, we sat on my bed. But just as we were restarting our abruptly disconnected conversation, Queen came to the room.

"So, what's the celebration for? No work tonight, eh?"

Nilofer and I looked at each other. Surprisingly I took the lead, "Queen … I have a request."

"What?" she asked rudely.

"I know we are not best friends. I know you don't even like me. But somewhere we are all in the same state of destitute—"

Queen cut me short. "Come to the point! And for your information, I don't think I am destitute," she snapped.

"Okay, I am sorry. I just wanted you to grant me and Nilofer one evening from our own lives. Please, please don't tell Nanda Masi. We promise that from tomorrow, you will never see any reluctance in us. And you or Masi will never, ever have a reason to be angry." I looked at her with expectations.

"Ha? Okay, just one evening. From tomorrow …" she said threateningly, but softly.

"Don't worry about that!" Nilofer and I said in unison.

"Okay!" she said, smiled slightly, and walked away.

"Thank God she is gone," Nilofer, heaved a sigh of relief. "But tell me one thing …"

"What?"

"Was that killer speech impromptu, or you had mentally prepared it?"

"Ha-ha!" I was laughing aloud after ages. "Believe me, I was absolutely unprepared."

"You must have been a great speaker at school, huh?" she asked.

The statement struck me hard, and my laughter evaporated. Nilofer was taken aback at my sudden change in demeanour, trying to understand which element in her statement hurt me.

"Oh, I am sorry! What happened Era?"

"Not your fault. I am fine, I am fine."

"Are you sure?"

"Guess so." I smiled, to her relief. "People like us have so many weak points that you never know when you might strike a chord unwittingly. I am fine now."

"I am riding the same boat, Era," she replied. "I understand. Come let's have tea. Queen's sudden invasion ruined our moment of frolic."

We sipped masala tea. Nilofer had some magic in her hands. Whatever she made, be it chapati or simple tea, it would taste sublime. The first sip rejuvenated me from within. Ignoring the slight pinch in my heart, I smiled happily.

"So, did you meet Ramanuj by the riverside again?" Nilofer asked.

"Of course. But before that, don't you want to know why your statement hurt me?"

"I do, Era."

"Well! It brought back the lost memories of a beautiful dawn. What a splendid morning it was!"

*** * ***

It was a beautiful morning. I got up very early to see the sunrise and sat on my bed sleepily, watching the skyline change colour like a chameleon. Generally, Appa never woke up early on Saturdays, but that morning was an exception. A soft knock at my bedroom door startled me.

"Era, baby are you awake?" Appa asked lovingly.

"Yes Appa, the door is open. Come inside please."

"Good morning!" he greeted with his signature smile.

"Good morning, Appa. You are awake this early? Unexpected!"

"True, your Appa is a late sleeper on weekends. But once in a while, the nature lover in him urges him to behave differently." He chuckled.

"Haha, of course, of course!" I replied. "Come Appa, come let's see the Sun God reveal himself in full glory, beating out the darkness of the night."

"Oh that was a great line, Era," he said enthusiastically as he walked over to the bed. Then he planted a peck on my forehead in appreciation.

"You liked it?"

"Yes, and I want some more," he replied.

The sun was about to appear, the birds were chirping, and the air had the sweetness of dawn.

"Okay, here I go:

Let the sun appear

Let the sun appear

Let it glorify my existence

Let it outshine all darkness

Let it infuse life into my worn-out self

Let the sun appear."

"Era, my baby. You are just a kid, and you have so much love for nature, so much creativity, so much literature in you. You make me proud. You must be a great speaker in school! No doubt you bring home so many trophies. I really want to hear you on stage."

"Appa, you just exaggerate ..." I said, embarrassed and hugged him tight.

By then, Ma was in my room. "So what is this early morning pampering from Appa, huh?"

"Good morning, Ma."

"Good morning, Nandini."

"Good morning, good morning. So what is cooking?" she rolled her eyes.

"Nothing really," Appa said.

"Okay, well, I will get tea for us and milk for Era."

"Ma, please! No milk, I want tea today," I insisted.

"Era!" Ma's eyes widened in disapproval.

"Let it be Nandini. It is Saturday," Appa said in my support and winked at me.

"See how you spoil her. Fine, have tea!"

After a while, she returned with three cups of yummy tea and biscuits. We all sat on my bed and talked our hearts out with steaming cups of tea, in the soft, sweet morning air, with singing birds for company.

* * *

"The glory of that beautiful dawn has remained with me. However bad things get, this memory will always breathe fresh air into my lungs," I said and wiped off the teardrops.

"How beautiful it must have been—sedate, glorious," Nilofer reflected.

"Yeah. Hey, I want to have another cup of tea, please!"

"Sure," she smiled.

We both darted towards the kitchen. Soon, we returned to my room with two more cups of tea.

"This day is really strange; don't you think so?" I asked.

"Yup," she replied.

"I mean, we have been together for quite some time now. Yet, we knew nothing of each other's lives before today. We knew nothing about Queen or Rosy. We just adjusted with our surroundings, completely forgetting the fact that life is not necessarily as discernible."

"Correct, Era. Well, I really want to know your tale. Your parents, your Ramanuj ... everything seems too perfect for something to go wrong."

"Perhaps perfection did not suit me ..." I smiled.

* * *

Ramanuj was before time that Saturday. We were expecting him at 11:00 a.m.; he reached at 10:30. His anxiety might have urged him to move faster.

"Good … Good morning, Uncle," he greeted Appa. I did not expect him to reach that early, so I missed opening the door to him.

"Good morning, Son. Come in young man, come …" Appa welcomed him warmly.

By then Ma and I had come to the living area. I gave him an assuring smile, while Ma scanned him from top to bottom. No doubt she was impressed by his appearance; her eyes said so. After all, it was difficult to dislike him at least for his looks.

Dressed in blue jeans and a grey casual T-shirt, he could have easily killed a million girls by his looks that day. But I restricted the bubbles inside and tried to look composed.

"Hi, Ramanuj," I waved from behind Ma.

"Hello," he greeted formally. "How are you Era?" This question could have burst the bubbles and made me laugh aloud. I mean … we had talked to each other barely half an hour ago! So I just rolled my eyes and said nothing.

"Hello, Aunty, good morning," he greeted Ma, who was still scanning him and was suddenly brought to senses by his words.

"Hmm? Good morning … yes," she fumbled. "Come sit. What do you like—tea, coffee or milk?"

"Coffee," he replied promptly.

"Okay." Ma turned to Appa and said, "Suresh make him comfortable while I get coffee and breakfast for everybody."

"No aunty, I have had breakfast. Only coffee will do," he replied hesitantly.

"No, no. Have little. I have made idli. You might like it," she smiled.

"I love idli, Aunty!" he said hastily.

All that time I was quietly enjoying the togetherness of the three people who meant the world to me. After all, it was a treat to my eyes to see Ramanuj, Appa, and Ma being nice to each other. What else could I have asked for?

Ma jolted me out of my thoughts. "Era, why are you staring at him like that and why are you so silent?"

"Um. No … Ma, I will come to the kitchen to help you," I volunteered.

"No need. Do you ever do anything? Talk to your friend. He is a young boy. He may not like talking to us oldies for so long."

"No Aunty, nothing like that," Ramanuj smiled. "I have been deprived of a mother's food and company all my childhood. I would love whatever you serve and also your company."

I could see the mellowed expression on Ma's face, but she did not say a word. Instead, she hurried to the kitchen after giving him a guarded smile.

Later, all four of us were seated around the dining table, enjoying Ma's awesome idlis and coffee.

"So, where are your parents? Where do they stay?" Appa asked, chewing on a mouthful of idlis.

"Um, my father, Dr Shankar Krishnamurti, is a famous heart surgeon. He is based in London these days. My mother is a psychiatrist, Dr Neelima Krishnamurti. She is in Dubai."

"Oh, don't mind me asking, but why do they stay separately? Is everything fine?" Appa asked apologetically.

"Oh no, Uncle. They are not divorced or anything. They are just different from most people. To them, profession is all that matters. I have grown up with my grandparents in Ooty. My parents have built a lavish mansion for us there, in the lap of nature. But unfortunately, it is just a mansion … not a home," Ramanuj replied glumly.

"Hmm. Cheer up!" Appa patted him on his back.

"And how come you are in Coonoor?" Ma asked; she had been a silent spectator till then.

"Aunty, this school is very famous, so my father wanted me to study here. I am putting up at the grand boy's hostel," he replied, a little half-heartedly this time.

The day went smooth, better than I had expected. After lunch, we all gathered in the living area and sat on the couches.

"Ramanuj …" Appa started. I kind of knew what he was about to say. The entire day, I had been anxious about this impending discussion.

"Yes, Uncle?"

"See, we are aware that you and Era like each other." Both Ramanuj and I were looking at the floor. "Though both of us know that these feelings are normal at your age, we want you guys to appreciate our concerns."

Ramanuj looked at Appa confused.

Appa started again, "I mean, I want both of you to understand the importance of education and invest yourselves in it and not give in to distractions. You can't have a life you desire if you don't build it on the foundation of education … so …"

"I understand, Uncle. I promise you that both of us will prioritize our education before anything else," Ramanuj replied with conviction. I nodded. However, I could see that Appa and Ma were not done; they wanted to say something more.

"Good, Son! But also …" Ma hesitated. "Um … we don't want you both to forget the boundaries of friendship. You are too young right now. A single wrong step can ruin your precious lives."

"Hmm, I understand." He nodded without looking up.

And the discussion was over.

A while later, Ramanuj left. I understood that my parents were happy with his behaviour, but his family background was a bit confusing to them. I cannot blame them, for the kind of societal background we came from, parents abandoning their children for their career was unheard of. Appa did not say anything. But Ma came to my room late at night as I was about to go to sleep.

"Era, are you asleep?"

"No, Ma. Come."

"I thought you might be sleeping. Era, you didn't ask us if we liked your friend?"

"Ma, I didn't feel I should."

"Okay ... but I am telling you voluntarily. He is a well-mannered young boy, very charming, attractive."

I smiled.

Ma continued, "But his family, his upbringing ... I'm not sure what to make of all that."

"I understand your dilemma, Ma. It is not too common to see parents choosing their career over their children. I was shocked too, when I heard for the first time," I confessed.

"Hmm. But I have a question," she said. "Have you ever seen any photograph of him with his parents ... grandparents? Or maybe a family portrait?"

I thought for a moment and then replied, "No, Ma, I haven't. Why do you ask?"

"Era ..." she started. "Era, to you it might seem weird, but to me and Suresh, it is important to know that you are befriending the right people. What apparently is absolutely normal to you, may not be so for us." She stopped to think and then added "In recent times, did

he visit his grandparents? Do you know anything about his parents visiting him?"

"Ma …" I scratched my head. "Yes, yes … he will be visiting his parents next month. He is going to Dubai."

"Okay …" she got up and started to walk away, but she stopped at the door and looked at me. "Era, I have trusted you. Don't break my trust. Don't do anything that you can't discuss with us. Remember, this is not the time. We can't and won't lock you up in your room; what we can do is simply trust you. If by any chance he asks you to accompany him to Dubai, just say no …" She sighed. "Okay, Goodnight, Era."

"Goodnight, Ma. And don't worry."

She just smiled, but I could feel her restlessness.

✳ ✳ ✳

"Era, you are the luckiest girl I know. Your parents are so different. Now I know where you get your progressive mindset from."

"I agree with part of that statement … but luckiest? That must be a joke," I remarked, "I mean don't you think, to be dumped in this darkness from a life like that is anything but good luck. Besides, don't judge my past so quickly. It is just the trailer; the movie is yet to come."

"Oh, I am sorry, Era."

✳ ✳ ✳

I could not honour the faith my parents had in me. Ramanuj was addictive. His touch, his smell, and his body—everything was addictive. Whenever he was near, my strength failed, my breathing quickened. I crumbled like a pack of cards. Was that love, was that lust? I had no clue what I was going through. My marks were not as good as they used to be before Ramanuj, but I was trying hard to concentrate and signs of improvement were visible. He, on the other hand, was a mediocre student. He wasn't like his doctor parents for sure.

That afternoon, we skipped school and went to the riverside on his bike. It was a joy ride. I clung on to his body, and we rode as the breeze flowed past us deliciously. I fell asleep and was brought to my senses when the bike suddenly stopped.

"Have we reached?" I asked.

"Yes," he replied, "Get up sleeping beauty."

"It is beautiful here, but I feel guilty for cheating on my parents," I remarked sadly.

"Love and guilt are two perspectives, weighing heavy on each other inside you currently. And it is true for everyone in love."

"But all parents are not like Ma and Appa. They trust me so much, and I repeatedly break their trust." I looked away. "Do you think I am a bad daughter, Ramanuj?"

"I don't know," he replied gazing at the water.

"Why do you say that? You could have just said no!"

"But I am just being honest, Era. It is a relative concept. My parents think they are right; I think they are not. Now you tell me, are they bad parents?" he asked.

"They are! I am sorry, but they are," I replied bluntly.

"Don't be sorry. But think ... you have just heard one part of the story, which is my side. You have never heard anything from my parents. Then how can you judge?"

"But ..."

"Era, there are always two sides to a story, like with a coin. And they never meet," he said and looked away.

I sighed.

"Anyway, leave all that. We are here for each other; let us enjoy our time."

"Ramanuj, when are you going to Dubai?" I blurted suddenly, a little annoyed by his bout of philosophy.

"Era, is this the question you want to ask now?"

"Why not? Look, you have met my parents. You know me inside out, but I never got to know your family. You don't even talk about them much." I was getting angry now.

"Then come with me to Dubai! My Dad is flying down from London too. You can meet both of them, talk to them ... do whatever you want."

"How can I come to Dubai?" I recalled Ma's words and was now feeling anxious

"Come on, Era. I know you can't come. Don't yell! You're acting like I have asked you to sleep with me!" he snapped.

"Ramanuj?" I rolled my eyes at him in anger.

"Okay. Listen, I am sorry. But you are behaving strangely. Don't you trust me?"

"Honestly, after all that you just said ... no," my anger spoke for me.

"This is ridiculous ..." and he was about to say more, when a third person spoke.

"You jerk, why are you fighting with this pretty girl?" the voice asked.

Startled, we both looked in the direction from where the voice came. A group of rowdy boys smiled at us. I immediately held Ramanuj's arm.

"Don't worry," he whispered, with his eyes fixed on them. "Let's go, this place is too empty."

In a flash of a second, we had boarded the bike and sped past them, while they yelled lewd things. When we reached the safety of the marketplace, we parked the bike near a coffee shop. The space was warm and colourful. Many couples like us had come there for a moment of cosiness and love. We picked the red couch in one corner, least visible from outside.

"What shall I get for you, Sir?" the waiter asked Ramanuj warmly.

"Umm, café latte. Medium. And you, Era?" Ramanuj asked.

"Cold coffee."

"Will that be all? You can also have chocolate cookies. They are fresh and yum!"

"Okay, get one," Ramanuj replied with a grin.

"All right, Sir."

When the waiter walked away, Ramanuj turned to me. "Era, the riverside is not safe, I think. We shouldn't go there again."

"You're right, it was pretty scary today. But it isn't like that all the time. We have been there before, and I guess this was just a one-off incident?"

"You think so? I mean, you are a young girl, and your safety is important to me. Remember that this is not a movie, and I am not John Abraham. I won't be able to take on the bad boys alone. For people like us, precaution is the best option … believe me!"

"Okay, fine, calm down! And I'm sorry for behaving strangely!"

"It's okay, Era. Um, well actually, it is not okay."

"Rama? What's wrong? I said I am sorry," I replied, both hurt and angry.

"No, seriously. I think you have doubts about my family. See, you are free to find out about me. I will give you all the addresses—Ooty, Dubai, London. I have not lied to you, Era. Why will I?" he was getting emotional. Thankfully, to break the tension, the waiter returned with our order.

"Here it is. Your order ... enjoy your moment!" he smiled at me.

"Thank You," I said. Then I turned back to Ramanuj, who was staring at the floor. "Rama ..."

"Era. I love you wholeheartedly. So it pains to know that you doubt my intentions." He was bubbling with emotions now.

"I ..."

"I know you do. And I will do everything to clear your doubts," he replied. "Okay, have your coffee!"

I knew the moment was lost. Tears were threatening to come cascading down my face, but I swallowed them.

✷ ✷ ✷

"Ramanuj sounds mature for his age," Nilofer said thoughtfully. "Very sensible and impressive!"

"Don't judge anybody so easily, my dear. We girls are extremely emotional, and often, that blindfolds us."

"And why do you say that?"

"Hmm. I don't know. Today, sitting here in this brothel, I do not know if I should have trusted Ramanuj," I said.

"Is he the reason that you landed here?"

"Honestly, I have no clue. But it's possible. I have an inkling."

"Don't trust inklings ... they too are often misleading."

We walked out of the room, the sun had almost sunk, and

the flesh market area was overflowing with prospective customers. The girls were looking at each of them with eyes full of expectations. I spotted Queen in a red, lacy provocative dress and cheap stilettos. Her red pout and overdone eyes sent inviting messages to the loutish men around. I looked away, and my eyes fell on Nilofer. She was crying.

"What happened?" I implored.

"We were happy with our frugal lifestyle, but Allah snatched that too. Why am I here in this brothel? Why am I alive? Just to die every night?"

"I don't know. I don't know if we are destined to find some good in this throng of ill, or is it that we are just ill-fated girls, destined to die a shameful death." My words only hurt her more.

"The latter is true, I am sure. I mean, what good can you expect here?" Nilofer rubbed her eyes and pulled herself back to reality. "Let's go inside and shut the door. Let the pandemonium of the creaky beds not reach our ears, at least for this one night."

We walked inside. There was an eerie silence for some time. None of us spoke or even looked at each other.

Then, she broke the ice. "What happened after that?"

"Huh?" Oh! My story of landing in hell. Yeah …"

✳ ✳ ✳

I returned home feeling strange that day. The plethora of incidents had left me a little numb. I was sure it also showed on my face.

"What happened, Era? You look disturbed," Ma asked with a voice dipped in concern.

"Um, nothing, Ma. I am fine," I said, avoiding eye contact.

"Okay, so when is Ramanuj going to Dubai?" You must have met him at school today?"

"Ah, yes. But it was only a very brief meeting. Didn't get a chance to ask him," I lied.

"Okay, okay. I will get you a glass of milk." She walked away to the kitchen.

My relationship with my parents had suffered a loss due to my romantic one. I could feel their anxiety and lack of trust. But we pretended to be normal. Ramanuj had altered my sensibilities. He ruled my heart and mind; he ruled my body. I craved to be in his shadow. His touch and his fragrance were driving me crazy. I didn't know how to reclaim myself from that mystic maze of fervour.

CHAPTER 9

"**I** have never experienced love," Nilofer remarked cheerlessly. "My acquaintance with my sexuality has only been gross. In this brothel, femininity has no place. It's commodified. I hate it."

"And I have felt the hormonal anomaly, but it ended in this brothel. Ramanuj was that dream that every girl wants to live, but I don't know why my dreamland perished at the feet of a nightmare. I don't even know if that nightmare was actually Ramanuj himself. It's all so nebulous that you can't catch the truth." I sighed and looked away.

"What happened? Tell me."

And I was back in my past again.

✷ ✷ ✷

Next morning, I went to school, still feeling unsure of the range of emotions inside me.

"Good morning, Era," Ramanuj greeted me at the school gate.

"Morning," I responded drearily.

"Oh dear. You are still so sad. I am sorry. I know I have hurt you. But I have realized that your inquisitiveness or doubts regarding my background are valid. So today, I will tell you everything and also show you the pictures of my family members. Happy?" His eyes sparkled; the anguish had vanished.

"Yeah!" I smiled back.

"But for that, we will have to bunk school today. Please!"

"No, no, no Ramanuj. Not today. The teachers will complain to my parents again. Please try to understand," I tried explaining, but I knew I would lose.

"*Era, please. Just one day. I won't bother you again or ask you to bunk school. See, this is important, right?" he convinced.*

"*Um, Ramanuj, I am not sure. I'm worried.*"

"*I am there for you.*"

"*And where do you want to take me? Riverside is not safe, right?" I asked indecisively.*

"*I have booked a room in a hotel just outside the city. Half an hour's drive.*"

"*What? Are you nuts? God … what will happen if someone knows about this? No way!*"

"*Era, just chill. Nobody will know. It's far away. Leave everything to me.*"

"*But …" I started.*

"*Era, sit on the bike." It almost sounded like an order. Strangely, I always felt so helpless in front of him, too weak to protest. I could never decipher whether my hormones were on my side or his.*

I hid my face in his jacket and clung on to him, to be as invisible as possible. He drove me away to an unknown place. I had no idea where I was heading. When the bike came to a halt, I realized the unfamiliarity of my surroundings. It was a beautiful place, and Coonoor had emerged in its glorious self.

"*Wow!" I exclaimed, mesmerized by what met my eyes. The greenery, the mountains, and the looming clouds—it was a picture from a fairy tale book.*

"*You like the place?" he asked expectantly.*

"*Yes, of course. But where are we and how far?*"

"*You will be home by your regular school time, okay?*"

"*Hmm, okay." I smiled.*

"Let's go, I have a lot to tell you, and time is limited."

We went inside the hotel, a small and cute abode amidst the lush greenery. Ramanuj must have made arrangements beforehand, for the receptionist didn't ask us to stop. We directly headed to the third-floor room, overlooking the mountains.

When he closed the door with a thump, my heart started pounding. Pretending to be fine, I walked over to the balcony and looked around. I could hear his footsteps approach me, gradually nearing my demure self. My heart jumped up and down, and my skin felt hypersensitive. Unable to bear the madness in my core, I turned to see his towering body.

He was standing very close, and our bodies touched each other. His masculine fragrance was driving me crazy. I looked up at him, with my back leaning on the balcony railing. He smiled lovingly.

"Era, I love you," he whispered.

"I love you too, Ramanuj." I couldn't stop myself.

He ran his fingers through my hair and pulled the rubber band off. Softly, he touched my face, and I closed my eyes. I could feel his hand, slowly crossing my chin, neck and then lower. I wanted to stop him but couldn't.

The next moment, he was hugging me tight, "Era. I love you so much. Don't ever leave me. Promise me...promise me!" he urged passionately.

"I won't, I promise," I murmured in his strong embrace. "Ramanuj, please ... no. I mean ..." I pleaded meekly.

"What happened, Era? You don't like it when I touch you? Are you uncomfortable, Era?"

"All I know is that I love you. But ... but ... all this doesn't feel right," I blurted out.

He sighed. "As you wish. There isn't and shouldn't be any compulsion. But can I just hug you once more, please?" he pleaded.

I opened my arms and embraced him with love. Moments flew by, but we were engrossed in each other's presence. The sudden knock at the door startled me. I felt unnervingly anxious, just like criminals hiding from the police.

"Don't worry, Era. I had ordered breakfast. Chill." Ramanuj smiled at me and walked over to the door.

We sat across the small table at the corner of the room, facing each other. He was coating the brown bread slices with butter, and I was staring at him like a hopeless romantic. Suddenly aware of my gaze, he looked at me amused. "What?" he asked.

I shook my head.

"Miss Erawati Iyer. Stop looking at me like that. I feel like a caged animal. Your eyelashes–big, black—are locking me into your eyes." I blushed at his comment. "Now eat," he ordered.

"Ramanuj ... I love you like mad. Even if you killed me, I would love you and trust you. What spell have you cast? Are you some magician, huh?"

"I am mad about you too, my darling Era. But in my case, I have no question to ask. I know for sure. Your deep, black, dramatic eyes have stolen my heart away. Your smile can kill me any time and your long, black tresses disarm me with its black magic."

"Don't lie. Haha. Um ... today I want to confess something."

"What?"

"I was smitten the first time I had seen you. You ... you ... are a charmer Ramanuj. Any girl would fall in love with you, but I never thought you would be interested in me. After all, I am dusky, very thin. I am nothing in front of you. Why me, Ramanuj?"

"Haha. Who told you that to be beautiful you have to be fair? I know there are many prejudices attached to the idea of beauty, but believe me, colour is just a meagre aspect of it. You are breathtakingly beautiful, and the wondrous aspect is, you are completely unaware. Go look into the mirror tonight. Look with my eyes and you will know!"

I smiled at him, but my cheeks felt flushed.

After breakfast, we sat on the bed. I knew Ramanuj had a lot to say, but he was unsure of how to begin. I decided to help. "So what do you want to tell me about your family?"

That day, when I reached home, pretending to be coming back from school, I felt light. All my doubts, my presumptions, and my fears had vanished into thin air.

I almost felt proud of Ramanuj's parents, who had taken the pain of separation from their son to travel the world and carry medical facilities to the unprivileged. They had dedicated their lives to a bigger cause. And their work fetched them accolades, appreciation, respect, and most importantly, the satisfaction of giving back to society. But they were bad parents in the eyes of ignorant people like me. I felt ashamed of how I had perceived them. The pictures of his beautiful mother, to whom he owed his looks, with downtrodden children of third-world countries, kept coming back to my memory.

"My mom had apologized for not being able to take care of me," he had said with tears in his eyes, as we sat next to each other in that hotel room. "She held my hand and looked up into my eyes and asked if I hated her. My anguish couldn't hold me back for too long. Crying, I had hugged her tight and confessed that I missed her." Ramanuj's words were echoing in my heart, as I sat on my bed and recounted the happenings of that day.

A slow knock at my door brought me back to my senses. I realized that I had locked myself in my room for too long.

"Era, Era!" Ma called. "What are you up to? Open the door."

I ran and opened the door and greeted her with a smile, "Ma I dozed off to sleep … so sorry!" I lied.

"Hmm, come for dinner." An unseen, unheard but loud silence had crept between my parents and me; I missed our earlier equation but didn't know how to work towards it.

"That's really great. Ramanuj's parents are so noble," Nilofer exploded with emotions.

"Yeah, I thought so too. But everything is blurred now. I don't know what's true and what's false."

"Era, I don't know what is so vague that you are unable to distinguish between reality and falsehood. Maybe when I know your full story, I would be able to form an opinion. Yet, whatever I have known of Ramanuj from you … he qualifies as a good soul."

"He does." I was suddenly feeling claustrophobic in that sombre room. "Shall we go out of the room for a while? I feel suffocated!"

"Yes, sure," she answered, concern evident in her voice. "Are you okay? Maybe we should change the topic … enough of digging up old wounds! It's going to get us nothing but pain."

"No, Shahin. I am fine. I want to unload the baggage, just like you did" I smiled at her and looked at the swelling and blossoming flesh market on the street. "These girls, these outcasts … they all have stories—stories of betrayal and fortitude. I feel ashamed of the society that judges us. When will this double standard end? The men who entertain themselves look at us with abhorrence if our paths cross outside the premises of this infernal. We are like shadows, with no real existence." I could feel my lips trembling.

Nilofer didn't answer. She was just gazing at the street cheerlessly.

"What happened?" I asked to break the silence of the moment.

"Huh? Nothing. What's the time?"

"It's 8:30," I replied.

CHAPTER 10

RAMANUJ

DUBAI, UAE, 19:00 HRS

"Do you realize what the time is?" mom asked with a tinge of anguish in her voice and pulled apart the curtains on the huge window. Immediately, Dubai unveiled its majestic lights to us, and even in my state of self-pity, I couldn't help but admire the resplendent view from our thirty-fifth-floor apartment. "It is 7 p.m., Rama. How long do you wish to snuggle and stay with that, imaginary quilt of empathy, huh? How long will you hide from reality?"

"Mom. I am fine," I mumbled.

"Rama, besides being your mom, don't forget that I am a psychiatrist. Recognizing emotions is my profession," she reminded me.

"Hmm." I sighed and sat up on my bed and looked out of the window.

"Son, I can't see you like this," she said and walked over to my bed. "I know … I know what you feel. But it was not your fault. How long will you punish yourself?"

"Mom, let's not discuss this, please. I am doing what you want, right? I have joined the institution of your choice, and I'm trying very hard to concentrate on academics. But … but that doesn't mean I am no longer entitled to the melancholy, which I own with pride. Era is my source of life … she lives within me."

"And I? Do I mean anything to you at all?" She had tears in her eyes. "Rama, I am your mother. It is difficult for me to see you in ruins. I am not snatching away the heartfelt memories you conserve within. I just want you to talk to me. Just once … son, I am a therapist, a counsellor. I may be able to pull you out of the darkness that is brewing inside you. Rama, please." She looked at me with hope.

"Mom, I don't want to come out of this darkness." My reply hurt her, but she refrained from expressing it.

"Okay, Son. If you ever feel that you can forgive me and think of me as a suitable confidante, I am there for you." She patted my back lovingly. "Now get up, I will get you coffee." Heaving a painful sigh, she walked out of the room with heavy steps and her head held down. The sight made me cringe with guilt.

"I don't want to hurt you, Mom. But Era is that shelter of love that kept me going when you and Dad were too busy to provide me with any family bonding. I can't share her with you, Mom … or with anyone else," I muttered to myself and walked over to the window, feeling like a criminal.

Suddenly, my mind was filled with that expressive pair of eyes, and palpitation made me feel fragile. I begged for forgiveness. "Era … how are you Era? I … I am sorry. I am so sorry Era … I …" Tears rolled down my cheeks, and my vision became blurred.

The beguiling glory of Dubai floated before my watery eyes. The dejected, petrified face of Erawati appeared in that and gradually shadowed the radiance. *"Ramanuj … Ramanuj! Save me, please … please, Ramanuj!"* I could see her hands reaching for my neck; they wanted to strangle me, but I had no power or will to flee.

By the time, mom re-entered my room with my favourite cappuccino, I was drenched in perspiration and looked battered. "Oh my God … what happened to you!"

I could barely manage to get the words out. "Okay … I am okay, Mom."

"What do you mean, okay? Tell me, Rama, are you not feeling well. Shall I call your Dad?"

"No, Mom. Relax, I am fine." My breathing had started to ease, and the sweat drops had vanished with the gradual return of normalcy.

"Okay … but …" She wanted more clarity, but her interrogation was interrupted by Dad.

"So, what's cooking between mother and son, huh?" He smiled lovingly. "Oh! The prince is enjoying his favourite cappuccino!"

Mom, who was yet to recover from the shock of seeing my traumatized face, could only manage a plastic grin, while I was still meandering in my grievous mental thoroughfare. Undoubtedly, our expressions perplexed him.

"Is everything okay?" he asked the two of us.

"Yes," Mom replied. "Do you want a cup of cappuccino?"

"Yeah … if I am lucky enough!"

"I guess you are." Mom went over to the kitchen, leaving me and Dad in an inescapable silence.

I could sense his unease.

After moments of contemplation, he was the first to break the ice, "How is the coffee?"

A safe question to start a conversation.

"Great … really good," I responded, without looking at him.

Following this, there was yet another stretch of unnerving silence. Like absolute escapists, we both waited for the moments to pass and Mom to return.

My condition had impelled my parents to shift priorities. I could not tell if that was good or bad, but we had started being, or perhaps pretending to be, a normal family. Mom's consultation chamber was a room in the apartment, an aptly created space for treating ambiguities in the human mind space. But even during her working hours, she would frequently come to see me to ensure my well-being. Dad left London and joined us in Dubai a few months back.

As their child, I could never make out why they had lived separately for so long. Was it only professional or had profession encroached like a dark cloud of emotional barrier between them? Whenever my mind and heart were free of Era, these questions haunted me.

Mom returned with two cups of cappuccino this time, and we all sat down at the tea table at the corner of my room. The darkness outside had intensified, and the lights were shining brightly in contrast to the black evening. The three of us drank in silence, my cup of coffee a little too cold to be cherished.

"Should I warm yours?" Mom asked, reading my mind.

"No, Mom."

"Sure?"

"Yes," I murmured.

"Okay, now tell me what happened to you? You looked awful—"

Dad interrupted her. "Wait, wait … what are you talking about? Will someone tell me?"

"Just a while back, when I entered the room, Ramanuj was perspiring profusely and looked shattered, as if he had seen something dreadful or wasn't feeling well," Mom said, by way of clarifying the context of the conversation.

"Oh my God. What happened, Son?" Dad asked

"I don't know. I felt a little uneasy for a few seconds, but I am fine now." I desperately wanted to end the discussion.

"Son, don't take it too lightly. We will get some tests done tomorrow. Did you experience chest pain?" The cardiac expert spoke for Dad, and this irritated me to the core.

"Please Dad, leave me alone," I said rudely and walked out of the room, out of the conversation and their caring shadow. But I heard them speak.

"He will never forgive us, Shankar," Mom exclaimed, crying.

"Time will heal. Give him time."

CHAPTER 11

I was waiting for time to heal too. This unmeasured mix of guilt and love was killing me. "Was I at fault?" I didn't know. All I knew was she needed help, and I couldn't give it. I also dreaded that she would misunderstand me, and that feeling of helplessness, hopelessness, and bitterness was instilling an incurable scathe in my puzzled mind. My behaviour towards my parents was often a reflection of that laceration inside me. However, it was also true that I was never fully able to understand or connect with my mom and dad.

But that evening, perhaps they understood me. After walking out of my room, I took shelter in the apparent festivities that dawned on Dubai every evening. The riot of lights dazzled my whims to an extent that I forgot a bit of my melancholy. The view from the balcony attached to the living area was to die for. I shut all lights, quietly sat on the easy chair, and looked at the manmade wonder. Burj Khalifa smiled at my sorry state from a distance.

"Shall we sit with you? Just for some time?" Mom asked hesitantly. Her words broke my flow of thoughts, and I nodded in answer to her query. The tone of her voice made me feel bad about my discourtesy towards them. But I preferred to camouflage my conscience-stricken thoughts in the darkness of my surroundings.

Their expressions were not decipherable, and I felt uneasy in their presence. And as they were pulling chairs to sit by my side, I kept trying to gauge the reasons behind their behaviour.

"Ramanuj, do you want to ask us anything? Anything that bothers you ... anything that arouses unwanted agony ...?" inquired Mom. Her mannerism said that she had already guessed the questions, but she just wanted to hear me say them.

"Mom, what do you expect me to say?" I looked at her without blinking. Her question had goaded the simmering fire in me. "After years of living with the feeling of abandonment, suddenly you want me to uninhibitedly pour my heart out to you guys? What have the two of you done to build a relationship? How can I actually confide my pains in you? My weaknesses … my … my insecurities. What have you done … tell me? You wanted me to ask you, right? Then answer me."

Tears rolled out of her eyes, but Mom maintained her composure and replied in a shaky voice, "You may hate us for what we are and whatever we have done, but today we are here to come clean about our insecurities. We are not your confidantes, but you are our only companion … our son."

"Really, Mom? There where were your instincts when I needed you the most? And your loner heart … did it not ever urge you to be with me?"

At this, Dad broke his silence. "We are not perfect, Son. And today we want to unravel our imperfectness, once and for all. Then it will be on you. If you want to forgive us or hate us for the rest of our lives—we are prepared for both."

His words struck me like thunder. "Are there things I didn't know? Oh my God, am I ready enough to bear another blow of fate?"

"I couldn't be a good husband, Son. I am a failure in my personal life," Dad said. I had never before seen him look so helpless. My heart was thumping mercilessly. I wasn't sure of my ability to withstand the approaching revelation. "We were pretty young when we got married, and very soon, we had to deal with parenthood. I … I … was probably not prepared to take responsibility."

In the moment of silence when Dad paused, the numbness began to ring in my ears.

"I was immature and impuissant. I felt I was losing Neelima, for she dedicated all her time to you. And in that mental state of incertitude and loneliness … I … I made a mistake. I …" he was fumbling woefully. "I met another woman … It was not love but a search for companionship." He hung his head like a defeated soldier.

"Dad!" the word came out unguardedly.

"I know, Son. You will hate me for this … just like Neelima did." He glanced at Mom, who looked mortified. "Your mom wanted a legal separation, but my parents urged her not to. You were their only reason to be alive, she couldn't snatch that away … and at the same time, she didn't want me in her life anymore. So …" he stopped.

"So both of you decided to shy away from reality and bring up a child in a fool's paradise … right?" I snapped.

"No, that's not true," Mom protested. "My heart bled for you every moment, but I didn't know how to break the wall between me and your dad to give you a normal upbringing. I felt caged in my own emotions …" She was weeping.

"Neelima, you never said you wanted to reconcile. I have died innumerable deaths in guilt. One mistake … slaughtered all my virtues. Why couldn't you forgive me?"

Suddenly I felt like an outsider as Mom and Dad unknowingly mollified each other's discontent and anger. In that emotional chaos, surprisingly, I suddenly felt the satisfaction of having a family. However dysfunctional it might be, it was mine.

Their outburst continued for long. Although there was an indescribable pain of shattering the image I had borne for years, I felt better. The sublimation of that invisible bitterness between them was clear. I had never seen them so vulnerable, so humane.

"Mom, Dad. Um, can we be together forever from now? We'll work through our issues. Are you two ready to commit?" I asked out of the blue, driven by my childish whim, which had been buried for years.

They both looked at me aghast. Dad was the first to speak, while Mom's tears conveyed it all. "Yes … yes! We commit to you, and I apologize for imposing the side effects of my deeds on you …" Tears rolled down his sunken eyes, which had begun to twinkle by then. He walked up to me and hugged me tight; I felt the warmth I had craved for ages. I was not crying, but my emotions needed release, and I eventually obliged.

So, from being separated by distance and thoughts, we evolved into a family. A unity initiated by tears and sparkling smiles!

"Nothing is more beautiful than a real smile that has struggled through tears," Mom said through her tears.

I smiled at her, but my heart was wailing uncontrollably. "Only if Era had been with me. I could have embraced this moment, with all my heart. Erawati Suresh Iyer, wherever you are … be happy! And I am sorry my love. I am sorry!"

CHAPTER 12
ERAWATI

Mumbai, India 20:30 HRS

"It's 8:30," I replied before she read her watch. But when Nilofer said nothing, I asked, "Shall we make something for dinner?"

But she ignored my question again and started talking about something completely unrelated. "You know, before coming here, I had a lot of inquisitiveness about this world of flesh trade. Although I never wanted to quench that curiosity by being a part of it; nevertheless, my life here is like completing a project I had undertaken long back."

"Project?"

"Yes project. Back when I was Shahin and a student diligently studying to change her life and make a difference to the world, I worked on an assignment on flesh trade. It was titled 'Prostitution: A Tale of the Non-existing Existence'."

"Nice … and what did you find out?"

"It's very interesting, Era. Euphemistically referred to as 'the world's oldest profession', Wikipedia says that the annual revenue generated worldwide is more than a hundred billion dollars … can you believe it? Not only that, there are more than forty million prostitutes in the world, and that's the official number. Their legal status changes from nation to nation, or even region to region." Nilofer paused to recollect the facts. "In India, prostitution in brothels or hotels, child prostitution, pimping, pandering … they are all illegal. We are non-existent entities, and we don't have any authorized identity proofs. Crimes against sex workers mostly go neglected because we are just shadows lurking in the margins of society. Every hour, around four girls are brought into prostitution in India, three of them against their will. We are people without any rights.

Even as more than three million sex workers in our country are being deprived of medication, education, basic rights, and above all, identity, our country progresses at lightning speed, Era … leaving us in the destitution that we have always been in." Nilofer heaved a sigh and hung her head.

"Are you all right?" I asked hesitantly.

"No Era. Right from the Devadasi to the modern-day hooker, flesh trade has always been known to all but acknowledged by none. Don't you feel it is sheer hypocrisy? If we are unable to restrict trafficking and illegal sex trade, why not legalize prostitution? At least the women will be entitled to living real lives, not existing in non-existence …" She was overflowing with palpable emotions.

I didn't know what was better for the country or us. I wasn't equipped with enough knowledge or information to form a strong opinion. But I appreciated her thinking, knowledge, wisdom, and empathy. I moved closer to her and hugged her tight. I could feel her sobbing but didn't utter a word.

The leftover chicken curry from lunch was enough for our dinner. I sat like an inquisitive child, watching Nilofer make chapatis for the two of us.

"From breakfast to dinner, it's like completing a full circle. Yet I still do not know your entire story. Era, today is the day. Let's finish what we started," Nilofer said.

"Yes … you are right. Tomorrow will bring some new pains, some unexpected smiles, but today, the day of freedom, will never come back. I want to finish what I started, but the sad part is, even I am not privy to the conclusion. It is unsettled," I said.

"Conclusion is a relative state; yours may differ from mine.

You divulge the string of events, and leave it to me to draw my conclusion, unbiased," she said.

"Do you believe in intuitions?"

"Hmm. Yeah, I do! Cannot forget Ammi's intuitive power. She had foreseen the mishap. If only Abbu and I had faith, my life would have been different."

"Well, Shahin, I had received signals too. But my dream-laden mind couldn't perceive them. I was caught up in my own thoughts, seeing a future filled with love …"

"Signals—like what?"

✳ ✳ ✳

It was a beautiful dawn. The opulent mist of winter had embraced Coonoor with grace. The strength of the morning sun wasn't enough to combat the chills, and people had to put on some extra layers of clothing. It was the ideal day for our school's annual picnic.

I got up from bed feeling surreal. It was a dreamy day for me. For the very first time, Ramanuj and I could spend a whole day together, without feeling guilty or the looming fear of getting caught.

I brushed my teeth and got dressed. In my ecstasy, I hardly knew it was too early to get ready.

"Era, what are you doing?" Ma asked, perplexed. It was a chilly winter morning. She was still barely awake. It must have been bewildering to see me all decked up.

"Good morning, Ma," I greeted her with an effervescent smile.

"Erawati, where are you going this early?" Her expression made me aware of the time, and I started to scramble for a suitable explanation. "Yes, Era?"

"Um, Ma it is my school's annual picnic today."

"Well, I know that! So?"

"Ma, my alarm clock went off early, and I couldn't go back to sleep. So I thought I might as well get ready."

"Hmm," she sighed. "And why have you put on this lip colour, huh? It's a school picnic, Erawati, not a fashion parade."

I immediately looked at myself in the mirror and cringed at my choice of colour. I was never a make-up person; my exhilaration must have completely taken over me when I chose that shade. "Sorry, Ma ... I will wipe it off immediately."

Ma's interrogation had already killed half of my excitement. Her next question decimated the remaining gaiety. "I hope you are not going anywhere else? Don't forget I can always contact your teacher."

At this, I looked at her flabbergasted for the next few moments. I knew that my friendship with Ramanuj was always a point of contention. But I had never perceived this humongous alteration in our relationship. My mother didn't trust me anymore, and I was to blame for that.

I suddenly didn't want to go to the picnic. But throwing tantrums would annoy her more, so I answered her mistrust with a simple "no".

"Okay, comb your hair properly. It is entangled at the ends. Wipe off that awful colour and put sunscreen on all exposed parts. I will get you breakfast."

She spoke without establishing eye contact and was about to walk out of the room, when unintentionally, I called out, "Ma."

"What?" and for the first time that morning, she looked at me with mellowed expressions. But I didn't know what to say, so I mumbled, "No ... nothing. Sorry."

She walked off to the kitchen.

I didn't have an appetite for food. But I knew I had to eat, so with a poker face, I kept munching and gulping it down like a robot. Two slices of bread, a glass of hot milk, and an omelette. It felt like too much, but I silently ate every bit so as to not anger Ma.

She was sitting across the table with her eyes set on me. With many unsaid questions bubbling inside, she kept gazing suspiciously. I hardly made any eye contact, but I felt her stare. At that moment, I just wanted to disappear.

Then Ma said in an ominous voice, "Era … take care!"

I nodded. She sounded cold. I wanted to run up to her and hug her tight. But didn't know what unknown force held me back. "Why can't she understand me? Why does she have to be so tough all the time?" I thought.

Finally, it was time to leave. Savita had called twice on our landline, and Ramanuj had called multiple times on my secret mobile phone. But the hopes of having fun and fulfilment had vanished. I just wanted to retire back to bed and never, ever get up again.

Bidding an indecisive goodbye to Ma, I started from home. The pickup point was within walking distance from my place. But my steps were heavy and slow. I somehow wanted to miss the bus and get back home, to my room and on to my bed. With my head hanging as low as possible, I clumsily walked up to the bus stand, but unfortunately, the bus hadn't left. I could hear the muffled rumblings of excited kids from a distance. I also spotted Savita and Ramanuj engrossed in deep discussion. Most definitely, their topic was me and why I wasn't there yet.

This picnic was for classes 9 to 12. Similar outings were arranged separately for the other classes as well. Our school authority believed in clubbing kids in such a way that they had common topics of discussion. I was in class 10 then and Ramanuj in 11, so fortunately, we were put in the same group.

When I approached them, Savita and Ramanuj noticed and immediately walked up to me. Savi was the first to speak. "What's wrong with you, why weren't you answering our calls? We thought you weren't coming!" she bombarded.

"No, I was late. So …"

Ramanuj was watching me with a frown. He said, "You don't look fine. Is everything okay? I mean, you seem disturbed. Era, you were so excited yesterday. What happened?"

"Guys, it's nothing. I am sleepy, that's all. I will unwind as the day progresses, don't worry." I gave them a reassuring smile, but Ma's irked face kept coming back to my mind.

"Are you sure?" asked Savi.

"Of course." I added a fake grin.

"Hmm." Ramanuj wasn't convinced but didn't prod. The three of us headed towards the bus. The driver had already started honking, to collect the scattered kids.

The distance from the bus stand to Sim's Park, the picnic spot, was hardly fifteen minutes. We chose a three-seater, and Savita took the window side. I was in the middle, while Ramanuj got the aisle. Those fifteen minutes of travel weren't easy. I could sense Ramanuj's internal grumbling, and Savita wanted to share a million things. I didn't know whom to give company. And on top of it, my mind was still with Ma and our disturbed equation.

Finally, to my relief, we reached our destination. Sim's Park was a park-cum-botanical garden. It was one of the most cherished tourist attractions of Coonoor. Spread over the Nilgiris, the place is heaven for nature lovers. There was a wide range of flora and fauna, including enticing and colourful flowerbeds. A soft cool breeze was blowing, which accentuated the overall feel. In a nutshell, it was an absolutely captivating winter morning, which had the divine power of healing all woes with its mystic connect. And in less than half an hour, the place had infused me with renewed enthusiasm.

The arrangements were great. The school authority appreciated the responsibility that came with taking out more than a hundred kids for a picnic. The number of accompanying teachers was enough to keep an eye on what we were up to. Sangeeta Ma'am had also come, and I knew she would keep an eye out for me and Ramanuj. So we were mindful of that.

The day was unfolding deliciously. The dormant nature lover in me was basking. In some time, Savita joined me, with the breakfast box. We sat down on the soft grass.

"Hey Era, aren't you hungry? No breakfast for you?" she inquired.

"No, I am full," I replied with a smile.

"What, Aunty made you breakfast this early in the morning? You are really lucky. My mom just asked if there was any arrangement for breakfast, and then went back to snoring," she chuckled. "Anyway, now tell me why were you so upset in the morning? Did you fight with Ramanuj or did Aunty say something?"

"Um, it's not like that. I am fine with their scolding. But the lack of trust ... it is very hurtful, Savi. And you know the kind of relationship I had with them. This harrowing feeling of guilt. I can't take it."

"I understand. Teenage relationships are never acceptable to parents, and it is unfortunate that it got divulged this early. I don't mean to lecture you, but you guys should have been more careful. My parents, even my brother—they don't know about Abhimanyu," she muttered cautiously.

"You are right, but it's too late now." I looked away from her and stared at the blossoming roses and marigolds, with the hope of locating my inner calm.

"Hey, I will get another banana for myself. Do you want one?"

"No."

Her absence gave me another chance to introspect. I was trying to release all my pain in the midst of the breeze and gain some tranquillity in return. The flowers were looking up to the sun, the same way I have always looked up to my parents. "If only I could express my feelings to both of you, I know you would have forgiven me," I thought.

Ramanuj stealthily walked up to me and sat by my side. "What are you dreaming of, Erawati?"

"Huh!" I exclaimed, surprised. "Oh you? When did you come and sit? I didn't even realize."

"Um, are you all right?" he inquired.

"Hmm."

"You look lost. We had planned a lot for this day, but you ... you don't seem to be interested." He chose his words cautiously.

"Give me some time. Especially in a beautiful place like this, we shouldn't be miserly in giving time to nature. I am fine ... just a bit of solitude and soul-searching will help me." My answer hurt him, but I really wanted to be alone, at least for a few more moments. Without saying anything, he walked away and joined the boys who were playing cricket.

Ramanuj didn't try to talk to me again. I watched him from a distance. He was putting his anguish into playing a good game of cricket. He was a good player, an all-rounder, as they say. Their team won the match, while I won some precious moments for myself.

During lunch, I approached him. "Congratulations, mister."

"Thank you," he replied coldly.

"Are you pissed off with me?"

"No."

"Then why don't you talk to me normally?"

"Era ... I am not a fool. Sometimes you want me to be with you, sometimes you want solitude. How am I supposed to predict your temperament?"

"Um, today morning Ma was very upset. She doesn't trust me anymore. Our beautiful bond has been broken. Can you believe it? She thought I am going out with you, instead of joining the picnic. And I am to be blamed for this suspicion."

"No ... not you. I am to be blamed, Era. If I wasn't in your life, everything would have been fine, rosy, and ideal ... as it used to be. So, I am to be blamed!"

"I didn't say that. I don't think that at all. But I just wanted a few moments of solitude ... to come to terms with myself, that's all."

"You could have said all this in the morning, instead of making me feel so unwanted. We had planned so much for this day and ... well, this is not the first time. I think you derive some kind of sadistic pleasure by tormenting me."

He was being harsh, and his words hurt my already bleeding heart.

"You know that's not true," I said and walked away.

It took a good few rounds of 'antaksharis' and 'dumb charades' to reinforce normalcy in the two of us. And at the end of the game session, the malaise was completely gone.

Savi, Ramanuj, I, and a few other friends were sitting on the grass and talking. The topic was just shifting from school to politics to movies, when a young girl, slightly sleazily dressed for her age, walked past us.

"Hooker?" asked Shekhar, Ramanuj's classmate.

"I don't think so. It's broad daylight, and besides, this is a family kind of a place," Ramanuj replied.

"What's a hooker?" I asked innocently, and everybody including Savi looked at me, astonished.

"Really … you don't know what a hooker is?" Savi was the first to ask.

"Um, that's fine, Era." Ramanuj came to my rescue. "A hooker is a prostitute."

"Oh!"

"I get so irritated when I see these girls. I feel like slapping them," said Nisha, our classmate.

"Why?" asked Ramanuj.

Nisha wasn't expecting this for sure. "What do you mean 'why'? They are prostitutes, damn it. The scum of society!"

"But I feel we shouldn't comment without knowing the circumstances that forced them into the business," Ramanuj said. I really respected his empathy.

"What are you talking about, dude?" Nisha sounded exasperated.

"Well, my parents do social work as medical practitioners in different parts of the world. My mom is a psychiatrist. Last time when she was here, I had overheard her telephonic conversation about the mental health of sex workers. She was emphasizing on how trafficking, inhuman working conditions, and social taboo have impacted the mental health of the young girls. Don't forget, they are just like you. And just because you are in a privileged, secure environment, it doesn't mean you get the licence to comment on the ones less fortunate."

This shook Nisha to the core. She excused herself and left the conversation midway.

But Shekhar seemed to be interested to know more. "This Nisha is such a snob. Anyway, what you are saying is correct. But as far as I *know, it's illegal in India, right?"*

"Yes, that's true. After overhearing the discussion that night, I did a lot of research. I generally do not share this bit, but since we are talking … Apart from going through lots of open literature, I befriended a social worker from Germany on social media. She has been working with sex workers for many years … and you know, prostitution is legal in Germany."

"You never told me any of this!" I exclaimed.

"Come on, Era, you are a kid."

"What do you mean, kid? You are just a year older than I am," I protested.

"Still, you are very immature. Besides, I find it interesting to know about the different aspects of society, but it may not necessarily interest you."

"Okay, so what did you find out?" Shekhar asked.

"Well, what intrigued me are the arguments she gave in favour of legalizing prostitution," he remarked.

"Really … like what?" Shekhar was fascinated.

"She said that after legalizing sex trade in Germany, the physical and mental states of the girls have improved, for they now have rights. Trafficking is more controlled, and as a nation, this business can generate substantial revenues. Well, prostitution will always be a reality, existing either on the surface or brushed under the carpet. At least legalizing helps the girls to come out of the shadows."

"And um, do you think a similar arrangement can work in India?" Shekhar was pretending to be thoughtful, but he wasn't getting half of what Ramanuj was talking about.

However, Ramanuj was oblivious of the intellectual level of his listeners; he just wanted to share his findings. "Well, it is tough to say. Every country is different. And with the kind of societal structure and socio-political environment that prevails here, it's really tough to understand. Having said that, India is one of the most complicated nations of the world, with the kind of overwhelming diversity in culture, caste, religion, and factors like widespread illiteracy and economic disparity. So legalizing prostitution will help the girls and generate revenue, yes, but the social impact and handling of the law … that will need lots of expertise."

Savi, Shekhar and I, looked at Ramanuj with mouths wide open.

"Well, don't judge me by my interest in a tabooed subject. I read a lot on different issues."

"Of course …" Shekhar said with a stupid grin.

"But why do you read all these? Instead, read about movies and stuff like that, entertain yourself Ramanuj!" Savi exclaimed. "We are on a picnic, guys, for god's sake; this topic is killing me with boredom."

"Oh … I am very sorry," Ramanuj said, embarrassed.

"Savi, whatever is uninteresting to you is not always unimportant," I said. I didn't like Savi's dismissal of Ramanuj's admirable qualities. "Ramanuj, I am really proud of you … you are so mature for your age. Although you do not top your class, your general knowledge overrides that of any topper I know," I said.

"Oh really, Era?" Savi remarked sarcastically. She was in the mood to start a fight, but Ramanuj intervened.

"No, it's my fault, I shouldn't have discussed this on a picnic."

"He was definitely mature for his age … don't you think so?" I asked Nilofer who had just finished making chapatis.

"Of course he was, but why didn't you mention this when I

discussed my research?" she returned.

"I didn't want to think about it. His keen interest on the subject, that German girl … these were signals I couldn't decipher. At times, I wonder if Ramanuj's bizarre maturity was his virtue or vice. Sitting amidst lush greenery that day, his knowledge about prostitution didn't summon red flags, but my present context does," I said.

"Why? Don't forget, he was a boy growing up without his parents with him, and situations like that tend to lead to early maturity. Besides, he belonged to a family that was probably much more progressive than yours or mine. And also, you didn't interpret any weirdness when I discussed my research … why this bias?"

"Um, I don't know. I just want to forget my past."

"But that you can't. You can only come to terms with it. Anyway, what happened when you returned home? Was your mother still upset?" Nilofer tried to change the topic.

✳ ✳ ✳

That whole day was nothing like what we planned. Ramanuj and I hardly had any time together. So, on our journey back home, we chose a two-seater, pissing Savi off for sure.

"Man proposes, God disposes. The picnic is over Era …" Ramanuj muttered gloomily.

"Yeah, but my morning encounter with Ma had set the tempo for a sad day. I knew it wouldn't be a great picnic, at least for me. Sorry for spreading my melancholy to you."

"We are not separate, Era. And I believe we will have a lifetime full of picnics." He gave me a reassuring smile.

"Really … you think so? My conviction is getting blurred day by day. I cannot fight my parents, Ramanuj. It is the toughest struggle for me to undergo …"

"No, no, Era. You can't fail … you just can't," he pleaded like a child, bringing tears to my eyes.

The fifteen minutes of travel was over in a blink. We had reached the bus stand from where we had started in the morning. Gradually, everyone started deboarding. I was followed by Ramanuj and to our utter astonishment and disbelief; my parents were waiting for me. Impulsively, we looked at each other, and Ramanuj smiled at them. They returned with courteous grins.

While Ramanuj started walking away with his hostel mates, I joined Ma and Appa.

"So, how was the day?" inquired Appa.

"It was okay," I replied, low spiritedly.

"Hmm, you don't look happy to see us?" he asked.

"No, Appa, it's nothing like that," I smiled at him.

"Suresh, don't you realize we have spoiled her evening walk with Ramanuj?"

There was silence. Prior to that walk, I couldn't have guessed that we could ever be uneasy in each other's presence.

Appa initiated the discussion again, "And how was Sim's park? We have been planning to go there for so long … good that at least you had a chance to see."

I really didn't want to reply; my tongue was feeling bitter, as if I had a fever, but I couldn't hurt him. "Appa, the park was beautiful, we should visit it again." I smiled.

"So, you just don't feel like answering me, is it?" Ma asked, thoroughly vexed by my calm.

"Why do you think so, Ma? And what do you want to ask?" My tone was brash, not adhering to my general attitude towards her.

"How was your day with Ramanuj?"

"It was great with all my friends, Ma. Thanks to your mood in the morning, half of my day was spent in despondency, the rest was fairly good. Nature, friends, games … it was nice, Ma." I do not know from where I gained the courage of confronting her.

"Oh, so you do care about my displeasure?"

"I do. I know you don't believe it, but that doesn't change the truth," I replied.

"Suresh … have you noticed her tone? How much she has changed. How much?"

"Nandini, it's too late. It is not the time to discuss these things. She is tired, and we need to return home quickly," Appa said.

"It will never be the correct time for you. Not until everything goes out of hand," she said harshly and walked away hastily.

Appa and I were taken aback by her reaction. He looked at me and my teary eyes, and before he could say anything, I clarified voluntarily, "I was always with the group, the whole freaking day! Why doesn't she believe me?"

"Come let's go … you need rest."

✳ ✳ ✳

"So your equation with your parents was completely messed up, huh?" reflected Nilofer.

"Yes, absolutely. And it was a domino effect. So the process of messing up continued like a chain reaction. Anything or everything I said or did, Ma associated that with Ramanuj. To such an extent that after a point of time … living in that house suffocated me."

"Really, relations and emotions, at times, are so tough to administer. You are left in pieces," she empathized.

"Yes, but I think now we need to have our dinner. Shall we take the food to my room? I am feeling sapped of all energy, and I'll need some food to continue with my story."

"Okay, mademoiselle! That's what Ramanuj called you, right? Or was it senorita?"

"Oh, it seems to be ages ago. For now they call me whore, slut …" I couldn't complete.

"Let's not get into that," Nilofer insisted.

"Sorry."

Nilofer's chapatis were as delectable as ever. For a few moments, we forgot our walk down the memory lane and indulged in its taste. But she was determined to know my story, so it didn't take her too long to return to it.

"And … what happened then?"

"You know what; I was actually refraining from revealing any further. The shrieks have suddenly returned to my mind and are creating chaos there." My heart was hesitant to disclose the moments of my past that I had preserved within, even as my brain had accepted my present. I am Erawati, and I will be Erawati forever. Chameli is my masked identity, bearing me down with its encrusted shell. In my thoughtful state, I said, "But I will tell you my story today."

"No Chameli, this isn't a punishment. I don't want you to go through all that just to satiate my inquisitiveness. This was meant to take the load off you. To rid you of the baggage of emotions you are carrying. If that is not happening, I would rather not want to hear your story … please, stop," she insisted.

"The missile has been launched, my friend, and no force can hold it back."

"It's your call. I am no one to launch it or attempt to hold it back."

"Hmm."

We had finished eating by then, so we stood in the darkened corridor. Although the sun never wished to grace the forbidden lives in those dilapidated brothels, the forgiving moon did. Every night, it bestowed its luxurious silvery silhouette on the mourning souls of the damsels truly in distress. Sometimes in the middle of the night when I had fewer customers to attend to, I stood there talking to the moon and sharing my woes. I fervently hoped that my voice would reach Appa, Ma, or even Ramanuj.

Nights in brothels had a distinct feel. The drab walls camouflaged their melancholy in the claustrophobic grip of the red lights. The girls concealed their disquietude under layers of make-up. There was an overflow of lights, music, and euphoria. But there was no life, and that obnoxious lifelessness often snatched my breath away.

"What are you thinking, Chameli?" Nilofer asked.

"Hmm? Nothing in particular. You know, Nilofer, often, in the middle of the night, I sneak out of my room to stand here. I look around the place and wonder what I am doing here. The man inside my room is a stranger to me, then why is he sleeping on my bed? I feel helpless!" I confided about my panic attacks for the first time. She was speechless for the next few seconds.

"And … what else? Tell me everything."

"I start sweating, my lips tremble and I feel ... I feel weak in the knees. Zillions of my memories start floating in front of my eyes. I ... I ... often see Ramanuj. As if he wants to tell me something. I see Appa, I see Ma ... I see Savi ... they all want me back. But a heavy door closes in front of me; there is no way out of this infernal!"

Moments of silence followed. Nilofer didn't know what to say. So she just gazed at me, stupefied.

"Um, since when have you been going through these traumatic experiences?" she finally broke her numbness.

"From day one."

CHAPTER 13

"**M**essed up equations seldom fall in place. They just become more and more messed up." Nilofer was looking worried. She didn't blink while I was talking. "What are you trying to figure out?" I asked.

"Nothing, carry on." She looked confused.

"It was never the same again Nilofer. Never ... not even the last time I saw them." My eyes were teary, a condition I was trying to avoid as much as possible. But my inner strength had started to wither as I approached the most abhorred part of my meandering life. I recollected the hurt in Ma's eyes and in Appa's body language. I closed my eyes and let the tears flow.

"Are you okay?" Nilofer put her hand on my shoulder.

"No," I answered in all honesty. "I had skipped tuition that day. The situation in my house was driving me crazy, and I needed to be at peace with my thoughts for some time."

✶ ✶ ✶

"You look so tensed!" exclaimed Ramanuj. We were sitting in the coffee shop, completely aware that we could be spotted at any moment, and the consequences would be dire. "Shall we go away from here? It is nerve-wracking to sit here when the only thing we are worried about is getting caught. You won't be able to relax, Era. And you desperately need to calm your senses."

"I know. But where do we go?" I asked, genuinely clueless.

"Um, let's go to the riverside, Era." He did not sound completely confident of his own proposal.

"But after that incident, we decided never to go there. And look around, it's a similar day ... the clouds are menacing, and it's just

about to pour. Rama, I don't think it is a good idea!"

"Yes, we did decide. But Era, don't you think it's absolutely irrational? It was just a one-off incident and shouldn't be the deciding factor for us. What do you say?" he asked.

"Okay, but do you have your bike?"

"Of course."

We started off reluctantly. Hiding my face with a scarf, I clung on to him, while the bike sped past the city and gradually entered the secluded riverside. The sky was grey, but it wasn't raining yet. The wind was fiendish, and the water swelled in anguish. The very sight sent chills down my spine. I wanted to return immediately.

"Ramanuj, there is no one. I am just not comfortable. Please, Rama, let us go back from here," I pleaded.

"Era, relax. I am here with you, and you are right, there is no one. There is no one to be afraid of."

"What do you mean ... no one to be afraid of? This expanse is so intimidating. I can't breathe. There is a strange warning in the air. I beg of you ... please ... let us go," I was restless. An inexplicable fright had taken over me; I just wanted to leave. But Ramanuj was behaving rather weird that day. Either he overlooked or belittled my anxiety, or there was something else that I could not recognize.

"Okay, calm down. Let's just sit for some time and then we will go," he urged.

I gave in unwillingly, and we walked over to the place where we generally sat.

"Wait," I urged. "We shouldn't sit away from the bike. It's our only ray of hope."

"Oh God, Era. Don't you think you are overreacting?" Rama was losing his patience.

"Maybe! But I think at this eerie riverside, anyone would have acted the way I am," I said.

"See Era, we are here for you. If this is making you so nervous, let's just leave." I could hear the simmering rage in his voice.

"Ok, Rama. We will sit for half an hour and then leave, fine?"

"Sure, mademoiselle!" He smiled.

We were sitting under that tree, where we had met for the first time. A storm of memories came rushing back; we cuddled and just basked in each other's embrace. Time flew by, and we crossed the deadline of half an hour.

Suddenly, an unfamiliar noise broke the silence. My heart had jumped to my mouth; I looked at Ramanuj. He looked tensed too.

The next thing I knew, there was a hand over my mouth. Someone landed a blow on Ramanuj's head. He was not fully unconscious but incapacitated. I could see his futile attempts to rise to his feet, while two men dragged me to an SUV parked close to his bike. I struggled to free myself, but nothing was working. I felt as if I was paralyzed. My vision became blurry and my body lost all its strength.

And then, the door closed. I caught one last glimpse of Ramanuj—lying under the tree, the tree that bore our memories. Drenched in the rain, he was looking at me, straight into my eyes. But I couldn't read the expression on his face.

✳ ✳ ✳

As I narrated what transpired that fateful day, it almost felt like I was reliving every moment. My heart was racing, and I felt like I would die. Having told my story also created a strange void inside, and my tears refused to stop. All this time, I had kept these memories at the back of my head. I hadn't recounted that event because I didn't want to acknowledge it.

I was living in denial. I would often imagine that my present was actually a dream, a nightmare … and that I would wake up to find myself still in my home, safe from the ugly ways of Kamathipura. A zillion thoughts blocked my senses, and I found it difficult to breathe.

"Era … Era!" Nilofer shook me vigorously. "What has happened to you? You are looking pale … shall I take you to the doctor?"

I looked at her as I regained my senses. My vision was gradually clearing, as if I was nearing the exit of a tunnel. "No, I will be fine. Give me … give me some time," I requested.

"Of course. Come, let me take you to your room. Rest for some time. Your mind needs to calm down."

"No, I will go to the bathroom and pour some water on my head."

"Okay." She watched me walk away with faltering steps but didn't utter a word.

After half an hour or so, I returned, feeling better. Nilofer was sitting on the floor of the open corridor, with her head resting on her knees. My approach broke her thoughts; she was anxious to know if I was fine.

"I am fine, Nilofer," I assured with a mellow smile.

"Thank God," she heaved a sigh of relief. "I was feeling like a criminal to have forced you into telling your story." Nilofer got up and gave me a tight hug. "Era, you are my Eos in this dark infernal. I really care for you."

"Me too," I smiled back at her.

She hesitated. "Um, Era. I must tell you this … you have been unfair to Ramanuj by doubting his intentions. He was too injured to have rescued you."

"Nilofer, it's not without reason. You tell me, why was his expression so blank when I last saw him? Why didn't he even try to get up to fight those goons? Why did he insist on going to that place even though I didn't want to? Why was he so indifferent to my uneasiness, to my discomfort? It's complicated. I can't really think clearly. And the inconsolable part is my inability to reach out to him and clarify my doubts … once and for all." I looked away. "Besides, there are more reasons for my doubts."

Nilofer looked at me, expecting me to carry on.

✳ ✳ ✳

When I was brought to Kamathipura, I wasn't in my senses. My vision was blurred, and my head was as heavy as a stone. They had probably used chloroform on me. There was a weird numbness and pain in my body. I couldn't decipher a bit of what was going on and had no clue as to how long I had been lying there, with that tape on my lips — hands and legs all tied up. When I opened my eyes, the first person I saw was Nanda Masi.

Her demeanour aroused hatred in me, almost immediately. She was atrocious, her beetle-stained teeth and obnoxious air was intolerable to me.

"This one is dark. But what a beauty." She smiled at me, exposing her red teeth further, and pulled the tape off my mouth. I looked away disgusted. "She will get many customers."

All the men around her looked at me and scrutinized me, trying to gauge my potential as a prostitute. They had a strange air of victory around them; I wondered what it was about.

"Who are you all? Where is Ramanuj?" I shrieked in panic.

"Calm down, child," assured Nanda Masi.

"Shut up. I want to go back to Ma and Appa … leave me alone!" At this, I received the first slap from her.

"You keep your little mouth shut." She rolled her eyes in anger. "Or I will break it! Look at her audacity … shushing me!"

Her violence shook me to the core. I started wailing in despair. "Please let me go … please! I am sorry … I will not shout at you. Please let me go." My left cheek was burning just like my sinking heart. I knew they wouldn't let me go, but my heart refused to accept this reality.

"No one goes out of this place, my darling," she mocked me.

"Why did you get me here … why?"

"Because we thought you will be profitable!" She laughed.

"But … I … I am …" I couldn't finish my words. I thought I must be dreaming, but the next moment, I knew that I was not. The insensitivity around was driving me crazy. I was hysterical, throwing my hands and legs and shrieking, "Let me go … I won't stay here. Ramanuj, Appa, and Ma—they will put you behind bars! I can't stay here."

"Oh, this rat is too noisy. Who is Ramanuj? The boy you were larking with? Haha, he's the one who sold you to us, stupid girl!" Nanda Masi laughed cruelly, and the men joined her.

"You are lying. You are such a bad woman. You are lying … tell me the truth!"

"Shut up. You squeaky rat." Then she turned to her men and said, "Take this idiot to her room and shut all doors and windows. Don't give her food or water as long as she doesn't learn to behave."

"No … no … no!" I kept yelling.

My cries fell on deaf ears.

CHAPTER 14

"Do you believe her, Era?" Nilofer asked.

"I don't know. I really don't … it's just that I don't trust my own senses any more. And I haven't slept in peace since then." I was struggling to stop my tears. "Every night brings a new demon. Sometimes, I see Ramanuj standing by my bed and ridiculing my innocence; sometimes, he asks for forgiveness; sometimes, he cries for me and begs me to trust him." I looked at Nilofer, who listened to me dumbfounded. "Nilofer, there is only darkness at the end of this tunnel. I am continuously getting charred in the flame of ambivalence. And it is excruciatingly painful. This pain is engulfing my sanity."

"Well, firstly, Era, you cannot trust Nanda Masi. She is an evil woman, who will go to any extent to break our spirits. Which I see she has accomplished in doing. And more importantly, you need to see a psychiatrist. The brothel's ambience is enough to make anyone go crazy, and you have additional demons to bother you. We should do something before it is too late, Era."

"Do you think we will be allowed? Here, it is okay to be insane as long as our bodies keep bringing in business."

"Don't be so harsh on yourself, Era. We can at least try." She sounded hopeful.

I looked away. There was silence for the next few moments. Then, I broke the monotony of the scary stillness. "Nilofer, I don't know if she lied to me about Ramanuj's involvement in my abduction, but I know how profound the impact was … of what she said. I was never the same again. My feelings were massacred, and faith was trampled on mercilessly," I said with a clenched fist. "If I come to know that she lied, I will kill her for the mental torture she subjected me to … I will kill her."

Nilofer looked at me with concern. "Calm down, Era," she

beseeched. She forced me to sit down, and we deliberately kept quiet for some time. It wasn't too late by Mumbai standards—11:00 p.m. The lanes of Kamathipura were busy and buzzing. We sat silently in the darkness of the corridor and watched. Tipsy customers walked hand-in-hand with the girls. There was no dearth of PDA. The girls appeared like mannequins to us. Many of them were high on drugs or alcohol. They probably needed to be high to endure the night.

"What do you see?" Nilofer asked.

"Despair," I shrugged. "And you?"

"Hope," she answered, with twinkling eyes.

"How and where?"

"There … in the middle of the streets." She pointed a finger.

"Nilo …" I couldn't finish. I had no energy left in me to argue with her.

"Yes, Era … Chameli … whoever we are, it doesn't matter. Think. Why are we in pain? Because we believe we have lost our dignity, isn't it?"

I nodded.

"But is it correct to believe that our dignity resides solely in our bodies and that denuding them takes our solemnity away from us? Are we just our bodies? Isn't there anything more to us … our nobility?" Her conviction was infectious. "Era, have Nanda Masi's vicious endeavours altered you from within? Aren't you still the girl that your parents brought up with their love and care?"

"Yes, I am that same old Era. Always Era," I replied with conviction.

"Good. Then why don't we do something for these girls, this

lifelessness? We have education to impart; at least we can help them find a way out of this darkness of ignorance. Whatever we know…whatever little we know … don't you think we should share? This way we can add some colour to this life of despair."

"Yes, we can … but—" An unexpected noise stopped me mid-sentence. "What's the hullabaloo?"

"I have no idea. Let's go and find out," Nilofer replied.

We headed towards the corner of the corridor that overlooked the stairs. When we reached there, we could see the origin of the ruckus. It was Nanda Masi returning from her day-long exile at the police station. She looked wrecked, her hair was messy, and her body emanated rage and weariness. Surely, she had had a bad day, and to reinstate stability, she had intoxicated herself with alcohol and drugs. She stumbled and slurred.

"It's okay, Nanda Masi. They will never reach her. This place is a black hole. If you get near it, you just vanish," her tipsy companion, who also happened to be her most trusted pimp, consoled her. His animated gestures and slurring exposed his own insobriety.

"Pfft!" Nanda Masi said. "This girl has been a pain ever since she arrived. Stupid creature! Always howling and always sick. A worthless piece of shit."

"True. And her parents…they just won't let go. Even today, they are hoping to get their daughter back. Idiots!" added another drunken pimp.

"And what will they get back? Huh?" she asked the guys with exasperation. "A hardened prostitute?" At this, all of them laughed menacingly.

"Who are they talking about?" I whispered into Nilofer's ears.

"I don't know. It can be any of us," she replied. "Um, Era, do you think they are discussing you?" I was thinking the same thing. After all, I was never a complacent inmate in Nanda Masi's prison.

"Yes, I am sure, Nilofer! I am sure. Ma and Appa must be here in Mumbai. This means they haven't given up on me. I knew it … I knew it!" I exclaimed.

"Shh," she said, a finger on her lips. "Do you want her to hear us? Keep quiet!"

"Nilofer, do you think my parents gave her a hard time at the police station today?" I asked with hope and a tinge of sadistic pleasure. In my excitement, I was still speaking loudly enough for my voice to reach Nanda Masi's drunken ears.

"Oh God! Era, shut up, will you?" Nilofer begged. But unfortunately, it was too late, and the damage was done.

"Who is murmuring there?" she asked, and her query froze our blood. There was an eerie silence after that. She was waiting for a reply, but we didn't speak. "Who is there? Come out immediately, or I will pull you out by your hair!" she threatened.

Nilofer and I looked at each other, petrified. Culpability blurred my vision; it was my irresponsible behaviour that had dragged both of us into this. But there was no time to introspect. We knew we had no escape.

Our steps were slow and unsure as we walked towards Nanda Masi. Her gaze was fixed on me. She was visibly gulping down a tsunami of rage, and her eyes burnt in the flame of her anger. Her jaw-line had hardened, making it tough for her to speak. The manner in which she studied me, confirmed my suspicion. It must be my family that had kept her in police custody that day.

"Why are you here? And from what I see, I understand, you didn't work today? Why, what is the occasion?" Her tone was menacing.

The silent, hostile communication between us didn't leave me with enough courage to cook up a story to justify why we had not worked.

Nilofer spoke, "Um, Nanda Masi—"

"Yes, I am waiting," Nanda Masi said.

"Chameli was very sick since morning. You were not there, and someone needed to take care of her, so … Masi, we will work religiously from tomorrow," she said, with an audible tremble in her voice.

"Hmm." Her gaze was still fixed on me. "What happened to Chameli?"

"Masi …" Nilofer started.

"Shh … I want Chameli to answer. What is wrong with you?"

"Umm … Masi … umm. I was nauseated and feverish. I felt weak and light-headed. I … I …" I pathetically searched for convincing words.

"Shut up both of you," she roared. "Shut up! The two of you will not get any food for the next two days and … and … you will have to cater to double the number of customers you generally do. I will personally look into it that both of you are tortured enough," she declared through gritted teeth, her fists clenched. Then she started to walk towards her room. But before leaving, she gawked at me, one last time.

We both stood in silence for the next few moments. When I looked at Nilofer, I could see the tears rolling down her cheek.

"I am sorry, Nilofer," I said. I was feeling extremely guilty to have dragged Nilofer into this situation.

"It's not your fault, don't be sorry," she smiled.

"We will survive this too."

"I am sure we will. But my concern is different," she looked at me with disquiet in her eyes.

"What's that?"

"I am sure you have noticed her resentment towards you. I am worried about that."

"Hmm … let's see what is in store. Maybe the worst is yet to come. Nilofer, don't overthink; nothing is in our control. Let us just try and get some rest. Tomorrow's dawn will be agonizing, and we need to prepare to withstand all the suffering the new day will bring to us."

We walked in silence. As we neared my room, she hugged me tight.

"Erawati Iyer, I am concerned about you," she said through tears. "Two days of hunger won't kill us. Besides, I have some hidden boxes of biscuits. And two days of torture, of being used, won't hurt our dignity … because those men will never reach our souls." She smiled. "But I don't know why this moonlit night looks threatening to me. I don't know what's in store in the darkness of this brothel."

Her words gave me goose-bumps. I gulped down my fear and pacified her, "Relax, the darkness will recede, and rays of hope will appear." But before closing the door to my room, I said, "Nilofer, if my parents are ever able to reach me and free me from these fetters, you will be rescued too. I will never leave you alone."

"I know," she smiled, and her eyes glistened in the mysterious light of the moon.

There was a meek ray of hope in that weird nothingness around. I couldn't make out what it was. But I knew that a change was nearing.

My wandering thoughts were disturbed by Nanda Masi's unexpected return.

"You are still here, both of you?" she spat.

"No ... No," Nilofer tried to clarify. By that time, I had stepped out of my room again.

"Shut up, bitch ..." Nanda Masi snarled. It echoed through the claustrophobic interiors of the building. "You two are crossing all limits ... you have no idea what you are playing with. I am fire and your hands will get burnt if you mess with me."

"No, Masi ..." Nilofer made another futile attempt.

"When I ask you not to speak, you must listen to me!" Nanda Masi's eyes were blazing, like a dormant volcano that had suddenly become active, ready to spurt lava and engulf all that came in its way. It was a different Nanda Masi. She had always been scary, but in that moment, she was like a monster waiting to devour us. The intoxication had added further fuel.

My heart was sinking, gripped by fear. I wanted Nilofer to keep quiet and let the storm pass, but she kept making one blunder after another. "Nanda Masi ... we were about to—" She could not complete her sentence. The next moment, she was lying on the floor in a pool of blood.

"Shahin ... Shahin!" I shrieked and dropped to the floor beside her. I slowly put her bleeding head on my lap. I was panicking. "What have you done ... why did you do this?" I shouted at Nanda Masi. "Shahin! Shahin, nothing will happen to you. Open your eyes ..." I was crying as if my last ray of hope was sinking in an unforgiving ocean of darkness.

We did not notice that Nanda Masi was holding an iron rod and carefully hiding it behind her own frame. Nilofer's words instigated the horrid woman to punish her for her obstinacy. And before we could even understand what was happening, the weapon had caused damage by one swift, nasty movement of her hand.

"Now you know what I can do? And this is just the beginning. No one escapes from me … and no one can rescue you!"

I was barely listening to her; my eyes were fixed on Nilofer's chest. She was breathing very fast, and I was dreading the worst. "Masi … please take her to the hospital. Please, Masi, my friend will die … she needs medical help! Please, Masi." I pleaded with folded hands.

"Shera … Laxman!" Nanda Masi shouted for the guards. "Where are you all? Come quickly … take this shit to the doctor." She pointed at Nilofer with disdain as the guards stood unfazed by the pains and blood of a young girl. Their hardened hearts must be used to worse.

"Yes, Masi," said one of them, while the other pulled Nilofer up from my lap.

"Shall I go … go … with her?" I asked in a trembling voice.

"Get back to your room before I slash your throat! Get lost," Nanda Masi shouted.

Before returning to my room, I looked at Nilofer once again. She was being carried like a sack. A trail of blood formed behind her. I could not believe what I had just seen. I did not know if I would ever see her again. Nilofer's smiling face, her words, and her tears blocked my vision. I looked at my dress stained with her blood and quietly prayed for her life.

CHAPTER 15

It was thirty minutes past midnight. I was lying on the bed. The old clock on the damp wall looked at me and asked me to embrace oblivion. There was a strange silence in the brothel that night. The streets of Kamathipura were not yet empty, but the noise was unable to reach the interiors of the disorderly house. Nilofer was right, that night had a menacing aura. Even the pandemonium of the squeaky beds had stopped for some unknown reason.

I looked at the ceiling fan and expected the monotonous movement to gradually lull me to sleep. But the continuous wicked thumping of my heart made it impossible for me to stay still. I wasn't able to distinguish one emotion from the other. I was anxious, I was terrified, but I was also hopeful. One thought concocted with the other and fabricated a complex dough inside me. Sleep was a distant dream. I felt that my heart would just jump out of my mouth and the veins of my head would just burst.

"Is this another anxiety attack?" I asked myself. "The brain is a complex environment, and most of the times, difficult to decipher. When the world thinks you are at peace, you might just be fighting the toughest battle inside," I said to myself in the uncanny silence of the moonlit night. "I think I can't sleep alone tonight. But I do not have Nilofer's shoulder to cry on either. Poor dear, my ineptitude has already caused her humongous harm. My dearest friend is in acute pain and misery, but I am so helpless that I cannot be with her." Her bloodstained face floated in front of me. I closed my eyes and prayed for her recovery.

After some time, I decided to give sleep another shot. The old clock was already reading 1:00, and there wasn't much time left for the cursed daylight to break.

I closed my eyes and recalled my days in Coonoor. Hoping that my fond memories would bestow some peace, and I might get some sleep. But I couldn't locate Ma, Appa, or my beautiful hometown anywhere in my mind space. The thoroughfare was secluded, unmanned. And at the extreme dead end, there was a door. So I walked over to that door and opened it. To my utter disbelief and desperation, it opened into the same brothel I was in. I wanted to shout; I wanted to break the prison walls. But then, I saw him—standing silently near my bed, head hung low in shame.

"Ramanuj," I whispered.

At this, he looked up. He looked exhausted; his usual strong frame wasn't the same anymore. "Era!"

My heart was reduced to a heap of molten wax when he called out my name. "Where have you been? I have looked for you in every nook and corner of this unsanctified land. But you didn't come. Why Ramanuj? Why didn't you come to rescue me from this life of misery? Why?" I asked, hoping to tame the rising tempest inside my heart.

But he just looked at me, without uttering a single word.

"Why don't you say something? There are so many unanswered questions bubbling inside me. Tell me Ramanuj, was it you who pushed me to this wretched life? Did you break my trust?" I was desperate.

"Don't you trust me, Era? Why don't you trust me?" His eyes were moist.

At this, I sprang up and found myself sitting on the bed with that old wall clock ticking away. It was 1:30. I looked around for Ramanuj, but he had vanished. Drenching me in emotions and perspiration, he had left me again with unanswered questions.

"God! I can't breathe. I need some fresh air." I decided to go out and stand in the open corridor for some time. But before I could make a move, I heard something. In the deafening silence of the brothel, I could clearly hear someone talking loudly. The voice rolled up to my ears like a rumbling, but nothing made sense.

I glanced at the clock and cross-checked the time. It was now 1:35. "Who is awake at this hour?" I thought. "Shall I go out and see? No, I shouldn't. This is a treacherous place; it won't be a good idea to invite further trouble."

But the voice had increased my unease, and it felt claustrophobic inside the room. After a few more moments of restlessness, I was determined to open the door and allow some air into my starved lungs. When I opened the door, the soft air hit my face. But nothing brought peace. The image of Nilofer being carried by those men flashed in front of me. Almost instinctively, I looked at the corridor floor and saw the stains of her blood. The view choked me with sadness. I knew I had to divert my mind.

I walked over to the railing and looked up at the sky. It was a clear, star-studded night, and the moon looked large and lustrous—as if it had jumped out from the page of some fairy-tale book. My breathing gradually eased, and the scattered thoughts started to align themselves.

I was trying to comprehend the reality of the facts of my life. A slight pain aroused at the centre of my chest. "If only I could be sure that the love of my life, my Ramanuj, didn't fail me, I could die in peace. I just want to stand face to face with the truth … just for once."

When the hues and cries in my inside had mellowed a bit, I heard the voice again. Immediately, my senses were alert. I tried hard to make sense out of the murmurs I could hear.

The sound was coming from a lower floor, and in no time, I located its origin. The lights were on in Nanda Masi's room. She was howling in the delectable silence of the beautiful yet scary night.

"What is keeping her awake? Isn't the witch satisfied after hurting my innocent friend?" I was seething with anger.

Although it was night, the silvery silhouette of the dreamy moon bestowed its light so majestically that I had to hide in the safety of a dark shadow, lest darker ones cast their curse on me. I tactfully glided and sat down on the floor but kept an eye on Nanda Masi's room from between the bars of the railing. I realized that she wasn't alone; her trusted men were sharing her euphoria over puffs and pegs. Their voices joined hers and created a hoarse pandemonium. The blabbering increased in decibel counts as the night approached dawn. I do not know why I sat there like a mummy waiting to be awakened. But some uncanny force prevented my body from making any move.

After a few minutes, the door opened, and Nanda Masi came out—perhaps to catch some air. Even from a distance, the claustrophobic, murky atmosphere of her room was clearly patent. The men were lying on the floor, completely plastered with the effect of alcohol and drugs. The atrocious woman, too, looked zoned out. In no time, she returned to her cramped enclosure but absentmindedly left the door open.

I was losing interest in that circus, and my body started to demand some rest vehemently. The next day could be demanding, even excruciating. I decided to oblige my body's needs. But before I could make a move, Nanda Masi's voice reached my ears. In the blaring silence of the brothel, I clearly heard my name. I heard her and the men say "Chameli". Taken over by curiosity and a strange courage, I decided to decode their jibber-jabber.

With newfound audacity, I tiptoed my way down the stairs. My heart was thumping like a notorious machine gun. I felt it might even be audible from outside. My lean body glided through the darkness, and I reached the nearest corner from where I could hear them clearly.

"She is such a nuisance," Nanda Masi said between hiccups.

"Masi, so many girls have come and gone. Why are you so worked up this time? These people will never be able to touch us," her friend assured her.

"And what makes you so sure, you overconfident moron?" she blasted. "I have handled many irritants, but very few like her. And to top it all, her family is hell-bent on finding her. I have to take some action ..."

"But Masi, why are the police entertaining these people for so long?"

"You won't understand, because you are an idiot," Nanda Masi shouted. "Obviously, they are either very rich people or have some high-level connection."

I felt a bit crestfallen at this proclamation; my parents were neither rich nor influential, so I likely wasn't their topic of discussion at all. A strange hopelessness gripped me, "So it's not about me; there is nothing to look forward to," I whispered to myself.

During that brief period of self-talk, I lost track of their conversation. But another mention of my name brought me back to their discussion. I focused on the voices again.

"Hmm. I could never make out that she was from any fancy background," one of the men slurred.

"Nay. Not that Chameli! She is from a very humble background. But that boy, her lover. He seems to be the son of some fat fish based in Dubai. His parents are some renowned doctors, I have heard," she remarked in anguish. "And it's probably them who are backing these beggars to continue pestering us. But before these idiots reach us, we have to …" Nanda Masi's voice trailed off.

I couldn't see her, but I could clearly visualize the venom in her eyes as she planned her revenge. "Ramanuj's parents … is she talking about them? But why are they helping Ma and Appa? Then, then … isn't Ramanuj behind my abduction?" These questions flooded my mind, and I was losing track of the conservation again. With all my might, I pushed the thoughts away.

"We have to what, Nanda Masi?" a man asked.

The next few moments were of a strange silence. I do not know what non-verbal communication was happening inside that room. The eerie uncertainty forced my heart to restart that rebellious thumping. But I heard them again, and their words curdled my blood.

"Lilac. Do you remember her?"

Her declaration echoed in the farthest reaches of my heart. I have no idea if those mindless pimps recollected her existence, but I did. My head was reeling, and my lungs were oxygen-starved. I didn't know what to do. "Should I try to run away? But how—how?"

"Hmm, of course I remember that girl. Ah! She was one tough nut. It was such fun to break her bit by bit …" One of the men replied in a voice dipped in lust and vengeance. His statement was followed by that wolfish hollow laughter I dreaded the most.

"Oh shut up! All men have the same one-track mind!" She shushed him and came out of her room, towards the open corridor. Her trembling silhouette looked menacing. From my hideout, she looked like a wicked witch planning to suck the lifeblood out of every living creature in her path. I pushed my body harder to the wall to hide better.

From outside the room, she declared, "If her family believes they can frighten me and take their daughter away from my claws, they are wrong! I either enslave my preys or kill them. But I never let them go! Hahaha! And my friend, death is not easy in this brothel. It is painful—very painful. Chameli will repay for all the insults that I suffered … hours of denigration, interrogation. She hasn't seen my real face yet. What I did to that Nilofer was just the trailer! By the time Chameli's family reaches the inside of this dungeon, their daughter will be dead!"

Tears of hatred and fear rolled down my cheeks. I could see Nilofer lying in a pool of blood with no one to help her. "Everything that Ma had preached about goodness and godliness was meaningless. What did I do to deserve this?" I thought. I didn't want to hear any more, I just wanted to run to my dingy room and drown in that nasty pillow, never to be awake again.

But I heard them again, and I was forced to listen.

"But Nanda Masi, why is the boy's family helping? Didn't the boy himself help you kidnap her?" asked one of the men. The question struck me hard. But even in that state of misery, I wanted to know the answer. I held my breath and waited to hear the truth.

"Hahahaha! Who told you that?" Nanda Masi sounded hysterical. "Really man, your brain is filled with cow dung for sure."

"But … but … I clearly recall you telling Chameli the day she was brought her."

"Of course, I did. Do you fools even understand how ordinary girls turn into prostitutes? The only way to prevent mutiny is by breaking their will to fight back. And that only happens when they know that they are unwanted by their loved ones. It's true that girls are often sold to me, and for prices less than cattle, but for girls like Chameli, the scene is different. Chameli wasn't disowned by her family. Those morons are still hopeful of getting her back. So to break her backbone I made up that story … to subjugate her emotionally. That boy knew nothing of our plan. We were keeping track of some girls in different places, and she was just one of them. It was her ill-fate that brought both of them to that isolated riverside that rainy day … that's it. But you know what? Era could have never been Chameli if I hadn't lied to her."

I closed my eyes to take the moment in. Ramanuj … my Ramanuj never breached my trust, my love. I was insensitive, foolish to have believed that vicious women. Sitting unarmed in this desolated infernal, I cursed his innocence for no fault of his. How could I believe her? How could she play with my deepest and purest emotions and push me into this life of degradation.'? "I have suffered more than you can comprehend, you witch. But I am still Erawati. I will never be Chameli. You should not have done this. No, you should not have done this!" My muscles were tense. I heard those men slowly walk out of the room in shaky steps. Then, after silence had befallen on those lanes of darkness, I stealthily climbed up the stairs to my room.

When I reached, the old clock on the wall read 3:00.

CHAPTER 16

I sat on the bed and broke down like never before. I cried like a baby, every part of my body shaking and sore. Zillions of emotions clouded my thoughts. "Ramanuj, you didn't break my trust. I am sorry, Rama, for losing my faith in our love. Forgive me, Rama ... forgive me! I love you, and till my last breath, I will continue to love you. Ma, Appa ... I do not know if I will ever get to see you again. The walls of this brothel will probably be my grave. But I love you both. I never wanted to hurt you, and I have never been an unworthy daughter." I sobbed and sobbed.

The clock was ticking in synch with my beating heart. I knew every passing moment was pushing me towards uncertainty. But all my emotions were submerged in a pool of anguish. I couldn't come to terms that the sole reason for my never-ending agony, mental instability, nightmares, hallucinations, was just a lie—a concocted conspiracy to break me. A lie that caused me more ache than the nights of torture, a lie that made me question my existence. A lie that was gradually poisoning my core and making me lose my mind.

"She shouldn't have done this to me. She shouldn't have pulled Ramanuj into her ugly game. I will not forgive her. She will have to pay for all her deeds ... she will have to!"

The last few hours of darkness were pulling me in its mystic embrace. I could feel that a different person was rising inside me from the ashes of my burnt, hurt heart—just like a phoenix. The new person was raw and burning in deep rage. She was neither Chameli nor Era; she was that disfigured mummy risen from the dead.

∗ ∗ ∗

I was hallucinating again. I could see him—Ramanuj.

He stood near the closed door and looked at me. There was defeat in his eyes. "You didn't believe me Era. You refused to put your faith in my love. That woman poisoned your mind against me. Is our love, our bond, so weak?"

"No, Rama ... Ramanuj!" I spread my arms to reach out, but he had vanished. Strange emotions gripped me, a transformation that I was failing to resist. I felt suffocated in my own skin. "Am I losing myself? Am I going mad?"

A strange voice echoed through the room, a young girl with bloodstained clothes squinted at me. She had bruises all over her body. I was terrified. "Who are you? What is this?"

"Don't you recognize me? I am Lilac. I am Lilac, Era!" My blood froze inside my veins. "They tortured me and left me to die. They are monsters, and if you don't do something now, your tomorrow will drown in the same pain as my yesterday. Act now, this is the moment," she insisted.

"B ... but, wha ... what can I do?" I fumbled.

"Everything is in your hands, Era." Lilac seemed to be in immense pain, and the words were mixed with an eerie sigh. "I seek vengeance. Ramanuj seeks vengeance. Your Ma, your Appa ... they seek vengeance. And Nilofer, what about her? Did she deserve this? And her family ... her ailing little sister?"

I had no idea of what to make of what she was saying. What did she want me to do?

"Era. Listen to me carefully! Kill her!"

"No, no, no! I can never do that. I am not a murderer ... no!"

I put my hands on my ears. I did not want to hear another word. But the voice resonated inside my mind, and I had no escape.

"Are you a prostitute, then? Are you that prey who is shared by the pimps in this heartless brothel? Are you that hunger-stricken, tortured, and violated damsel in distress? What are you, Era? Who are you?"

"I don't know ... I don't know," I shouted in despair.

"Kill her. She deserves to die. She deserves pain ... hatred. All these girls hidden in anonymity, in the forbidden walls of this dead, dark house ... they are entitled to justice that only you can render! You are the chosen one. You are the Eos of the Infernal."

The words rang inside me.

"Yes, Era, yes. She must die. Avenge my sufferings, Era." I could see Nilofer bleeding profusely.

The oblivion broke with my heavy gasping, my head was reeling; my dress was drenched in sweat. I wasn't myself. A beast had been unleashed, and I had no control over my actions and emotions. My body was rebellious; it cried for rest. My heart was burnt black with no remains of emotion.

As I put my shaky feet on the floor, I realized it was difficult for me to balance my footsteps. But eventually, I did. I stood strong, determined to end my tale of despair. The morning sun may bring ill fate to me, but it will free the fettered birds to fly high.

As my mind wandered around the untraversed lanes, my eyes fell on the clock, it was 3:20 already. And I knew I didn't have much time left to execute the final task. The new dawn was about to break, and the reformation must happen before the rays touch the walls of the infernal.

I searched my dingy room like mad. I clearly remembered that the last time we prepared chicken, Nilofer had kept the knife in my room. She was strangely fascinated with that deadly weapon and claimed that it cut flesh the way no other knife in the brothel's kitchen did. So, she had hidden it—to have a monopoly over its use.

"Where is it? Where is it?"

Going through all chests and drawers, I finally found it. It was hidden under the piles of paper in my personal compartment, where I also treasured the remains of Era. The sight of the knife pumped more vigour in me.

"Era is the chosen one," I thought aloud.

As I held the knife in my trembling hands, my throat went dry. From nowhere in that unnerving silence, some words came echoing towards me. "Go ahead, you are on the right track! And there is no looking back and no time to spare."

Taken over by an unearthly wave of anger, I opened the door and darted towards her room. My alter ego had strangulated Era's dreamy self and assassinated Chameli's fear-stricken psyche. It was a new me—a phantom, a protector, an avenger.

CHAPTER 17

It was that time of the night when darkness is most intense and silence most heady. The last few moments of battle between murk and light had commenced in full vigour. It was that moment of dethroning the evil and coronation of humanity.

My advances towards closing the scathing chapter of my life had started as I stepped out of my room and into the open corridor. I could see Nanda Masi's room, and it was sending sharp chills down my spine. But the phoenix in me would not allow the multitude of emotions to deter my conviction. My senses were on high alert and I was moving stealthily towards my destination. But my rebellious heart was stubborn and wasn't listening to any of my pleas to be quiet. It kept racing with every passing moment.

I climbed down the stairs and scanned the corridor thoroughly before stepping out of the dark shadow of the staircase. After confirming the emptiness of the floor, I tiptoed furtively towards her room. My body lacked human feelings at that moment. It was vengeful, and my eyes hurled fire. The anxiety-stacked nights, the sweaty darkness, the bloodstained dress on Lilac, Ramanuj's desperate cries to prove his innocence, and most importantly, that blow … that blow to Nilofer's head, her blood, her pain, her helplessness! All these had engulfed me.

"You don't deserve to live, Nanda!" The words resonated inside my mind.

I was standing in front of the door that led to her airless abode of treachery. My throat was dry, and my hands were trembling violently. "Go inside ... don't waste time," a voice echoed from nowhere. And my hypnotized self abided. I stepped inside the darkness.

When I opened the door, the skylight fell on her, and I could make out that she was absolutely sloshed. Even trumpets would not have woken her up. I silently closed the door behind me and patiently waited for my eyes to get acclimatized to the dim light of the room.

A strange anger had gripped me by then, and I was not experiencing fear or anxiety.

"I will sacrifice my innocence today ... that's what you always wanted, right? For all the sleepless nights, trauma, and torture that you have subjected me to ... and for all the blood that flowed out of my friend's body ... I will give you death!" I didn't feel an iota of hesitance or guilt. Abhorrence was flowing out of my eyes in the form of tears. I looked at the knife in my hand and moved closer to her. My dark shadow loomed menacingly over her. Her chest moved up and down. I stood there motionlessly, waiting to snatch that life away.

"Era ... Erawati! Go back to your room!" A voice echoed in my head. "You are not a murderer. Look at yourself ... with a knife in your hand and heart overflowing with darkness. Are you really your Appa and Ma's Era?"

"I ..." I wanted to say something, but another voice came rambling. I could see Lilac again.

"Era, don't listen to her. You are the chosen one. You must put an end to this inhumanity. You must sacrifice your innocence for this bigger cause. Look at me ... my bruises are still raw. And if you don't kill her, you will be bruised like me. Do not give her any more power to persecute you. She hit Nilofer just to prove her power. She must die Era. Stab her to death—dig your weapon deep! She deserves pain ... she deserves death."

Numerous shadows circled me. I do not know who they were. Shrieks were heard from every corner of my brain and I could clearly hear them. "Kill her!" I could see the shadow of my raised knife readying to slash her.

Then, on the count of three, the deadly weapon had penetrated her black heart. There was blood all around. I have no idea, how many times I stabbed her, but her soul had already left the impious cage of her body. She had taken a deep breath before her breathing stopped forever.

I was numb; my hands were stained with blood. Suddenly, all the shadows had vanished, and I was all alone in that dark, menacing room. I was covered with beads of sweat, and when I raised my hand to wipe my forehead, I soiled my face with Nanda Masi's blood. When I looked up, my eyes fell on the mirror on the wall. In that grim light of the room, with my open hair, bloodstained hands and face, protruding red eyes—a lifeless body on the bed—I looked like the personification of vengeance. I couldn't look at myself.

The muddled thoughts could not hold me for long, though. I knew I had to make a move. And so, in swift steps, I walked towards the door and carefully opened it. My state was dire and encountering anyone could be deadly. I had to hide my bloodstained appearance before the sun rose.

Before I left the room, I looked at her body—lifeless, helpless. "I don't regret killing her," I said to myself.

The corridor was empty when I stepped out. All the girls were enjoying their last few hours of luxury before Nanda Masi pulled them off their beds. Of course, they had no clue that she would never do that again.

I walked slowly in the dark shadow, avoiding getting noticed in case anyone was awake. I also discerned that I had to get rid of the weapon as soon as possible. My mind was racing like a seasoned killer's, and I shocked myself every moment. "I can throw it off the railing from the staircase and straight into the pond ... no one will be able to locate it there," I thought. Then I tiptoed towards the staircase. But before I could start my ascent, I heard something. Instinctively, I jumped to the side and listened keenly. "Yes, someone is awake." My heart was thumping like mad. Steps could be heard clearly from the floor above, which was my floor.

"Did I close the door before coming out?" The very notion brought sweat drops on my forehead. "What if this person checks my room and raises an alarm? No, why would she do that? She will surmise that I have gone to the loo or maybe downstairs to catch some air. There is nothing to worry about." My assumptions and presumptions fought with each other, and my bodily strength was gradually withering. With no sleep and unimaginable precariousness, my frail frame was losing all its strength with every passing moment.

The sound of steps was heard no more, but I had no idea if that person had gone back to her room. I knew I could not wait there indefinitely; I had to make a move very soon. And so I did.

One step at a time, I started climbing the stairs, and as soon as I reached the location, I threw the knife with all my remaining might. Fortunately, it dived straight into the heart of the deep pond. "Ah, thank god," I murmured. Then started my climb again. Finally, I reached the corridor and could see the door of my shadowy room. Strangely that hated expanse was luring me towards itself like never before. I ran towards it and slammed the door behind me as soon as I was in.

Resting my back on the closed door, I shut my eyes and let oxygen into my lungs. Gradually, when my breathing normalized, I looked into the mirror in front of me. I was looking devastated—debilitated mentally and physically.

There were bloodstains on my dress—a mixture of Nilofer's and Nanda Masi's. My hand and face looked like that of a cannibal after devouring food.

I cringed and immediately undressed. There was a small washbasin at the corner of my room, which mostly did not have water supply, but that night it surprised me. I washed my hands and face, then put on a comfortable maxi. I knew I had to wash my bloodstained dress too. But for that, I needed the bigger tap in the washroom and stronger flow of water, which was available only in the morning. So I hid the dress under a small heave of empty liquor bottles.

"Let me lie down for some time." I knew the next morning was unpredictable, full of anxieties and fear. I wanted to have what could be my last sleep in freedom.

I lay down on the bed, and I don't know why but tears started rolling down my eyes. I missed being Era and I was worried about Nilofer. A plethora of emotions choked me, and in no time, deep sleep engulfed my senses. My tired body had finally given up.

✳ ✳ ✳

I was startled by the sudden knock on the door. My deep slumber was broken with a jolt. I felt dizzy and unsure of my whereabouts. It took me a good few seconds to recall the string of events that marked the fateful last night. Almost immediately, I remembered that my bloodstained dress was hidden under the heave of liquor bottles. But it was too late to take any action.

My eyes were clogged with darkness, and when I opened the door, the sudden gush of light blinded me. Amidst that dazzling and confusing bout of light, I could see numerous faces, but I wasn't able to recognize any. Thoughts, dreams, diffidence, and fear had cluttered inside my brain.

"Chameli! Are you Chameli?" asked a voice. Gradually, the mess had cleared, and I could see the lady constable. But I wasn't fearful anymore.

"Hmm." I nodded in return.

"Come with me," she ordered.

I followed. As I walked through the corridor, all faces turned to see me. Strangely, I did not know that there were so many unknown girls in the brothel. But amidst all the unfamiliarity, I also spotted Rosy and Queen peering at me. I smiled at them, but they did not smile back. They had questions in their eyes, doubts in their body language, so I just looked away.

There were numerous policemen in the building, asking questions, scrutinizing the crime scene. The atmosphere was tense. I could hear the siren of the ambulance; Nanda Masi's lifeless body was being carried downstairs. It would go for post-mortem.

In that cynical atmosphere, when everyone had frowns on their foreheads, I was feeling hopeful. For the first time during my long exile, I saw sunlight peeping into the maze of despondency. I smiled and that grin reached my eyes.

CHAPTER 18

IN SOME JUVENILE JAIL NEAR MUMBAI, INDIA, 23:30 HRS

"Era ... do you regret what you did?" asked Sharda, an eighteen-year-old murder accused. She had poisoned her abusive husband when she came to know that he was conspiring to kill her and their one-year-old daughter.

"No, never ... it is not that I could put an end to the sufferings of all the girls in the brothel, but at least I avenged the agonies of a few, most importantly Nilofer's. I do not have any regrets. I prefer this prison over that hell." I smiled.

Sharda and I shared the same room and often discussed what life had made of us. Truly, we had come a long way, from innocent to accused, from tormented to avengers. We had gone through a complete metamorphosis.

After being charged with the offence of killing Nanda Masi, I was sentenced for seven long years. As I was a juvenile, a board of psychologists and sociologists had taken an interest in me. However, they eventually declared that it was a cold-blooded crime, and I deserved to be punished. But my age saved me from life imprisonment.

Since that day, prison became my home—of hope and reformation. I wanted to shed off all the dirt that had accumulated on my mind and heart from my stint in the brothel, and evolve as a strong woman, which an unjust, patriarchal society would not be able to break. I was preparing each day, to face the world. So what if the light at the end of the tunnel was really far off? So what if my days of confinement had just commenced? I was hopeful for a brighter future—a dignified one.

And the best part of being in jail was that I could meet Ma and Appa. They had rented a small apartment in Mumbai's suburbs and regularly came to see me. They inspired the agonized Chameli in me to be Era again—even better than Era, in fact.

I vividly remember the moment I met Ma and Appa. It was in the police custody when I was undergoing interrogation. They looked frail and tired, but their eyes were burning with hope. Ma had burst into tears, but Appa just kept staring at me without blinking. The plethora of emotions in my heart and the multitude of unsaid words that were exchanged were incredible.

"How have you been my Era ... my love?" Ma had asked with an audible quiver in her voice.

That was the rekindling moment of our prodigious bond. Since then, they have been integral parts on my path of reclaiming my inner self. It was sublime to be able to unmask my inglorious journey to them. I felt liberated like never before.

I had now been in judicial custody for three months. Confinement was claustrophobic; I did not have a life of my choice. Besides I had to share my living space with people I could hardly relate to. There were murderers, thieves, and all kinds of offenders. Some were truly menacing, and I was learning to avoid crossing paths with them. But some were not as heinous. They were victims of their circumstances and sufferers at the hands of their near and dear ones, until one fine day they gave back and landed in jail, like I had. Just like the dolled-up faces in the brothel hid many traumatized hearts, the contemptible exteriors of the convicts often hid tender, insecure, and innocent souls.

Life in prison was a struggle. Survival needed a strategy.

Whom to speak to and whom to avoid—there were cliques and groups inside the confined walls. One wrong step could land you in grave trouble. I was gradually getting accustomed to the ways of the place, and I had accepted the fact that it was going to be a very long and exigent journey.

"Era … My crime was just out of impulse." Sharda's voice broke my reverie. "I call it defence, they called it cold-blooded murder. I was petrified at the thought of any harm coming to my child, Era. I didn't kill him to save myself. From the night we started our married life together, he had tortured me. Yet, the thought of ending his life had never crossed my mind. But … but … I am a mother, and I cannot allow any force in the universe to harm my daughter. She does not deserve to die just because her father—her worthless, spineless father—wanted a son!" Sharda spat in disgust and burst into tears. I had heard her story many times in the last three months, but each time her emotions charged at me with the same might, I ended up shedding tears of empathy.

"Calm down," I whispered.

"Anyway, forget about me." She rubbed her eyes like a child and continued, "Era, I wanted to remind you once again. Do not … do not mingle with anyone without discussing with me, you hardly know them. Era, you are like my younger sister. I want you to be safe." After moments of pause, she said, "This jail is a strange place, and there are girls with varied instincts. Then there are predators—they hurt, abuse and torture. Absolute sadists … hardened criminals. Be cordial and respectful to all but close to none, that is the unsaid rule. However, even this decree can't assure safety. So, befriend a few who are in power … like I did. Otherwise, it is very difficult to survive. But do not worry, sister, I will protect you with everything I have." She had genuine love in her eyes.

"Thank you," I replied, inundated with gratitude.

"Um, Era. May I ask you a question?"

"Of course!"

"Do you ... do you miss him?"

The question startled me. "No ... he is with me. I feel him. He is around."

After a while, we both embraced slumber. Days were arduous and demanded a lot of toil and energy, so sleep came easy, unlike in the brothel.

O6:30 hrs

"Have you cut all the tomatoes?" the kitchen in-charge demanded sharply. "We have to start making breakfast. Hurry up, girls! There is no time for leisure."

Every girl in the jail was assigned some duty; I was with the kitchen team. My day started with chopping copious amounts of vegetables, then helping to prepare meals, and later serving food to the inmates. It was tiresome, to say the least. Standing all through the day and in not-so-agreeable conditions wasn't easy. I was new to the drill, and my body was gradually adjusting to the sudden increase in toil. Most days, my day ended with a cut on a finger or an aching back. But I was growing stronger and was determined to sail through. In the grave darkness of insecurity, I was unimaginably positive.

"Almost done." I smiled.

"Good. Now start chopping the onions," she ordered.

"Okay," I replied and immediately started with my next assignment. I knew good work and reputation could help me return to normal life sooner. It was my only ray of hope, pulling me like a powerful magnet.

"I don't need to instruct Era! Why are *you* so clumsy ... procrastinating and day-dreaming all the time?" my thoughts were interrupted by the in-charge's sudden outburst. She was reprimanding another girl, who was receiving the bitter words quietly, with a poker face. It was true that she wasn't good at her work, but I felt as if there was more to her silence. She looked weak and disoriented, hardly speaking to anyone. I felt bad for her, and for some reason, she always reminded me of Nilofer.

"I hope Nilofer is fine. She must have recovered by now. I wish she comes to meet me someday. I really want to talk to her," I thought.

After wrapping up all the kitchen work, I sat down in the garden area. Sometimes, in the scorching heat of Mumbai, I felt the chills of Coonoor and memories came rushing back to me. The dismal state of my brothel room visited the desolate thoroughfare of my mind again and again. But this was a new Erawati—hardened yet positive, a murderer yet innocent, gullible yet strong. Life had come a long way, and I knew good times awaited in the future. I had fought the worst battles, but no more. Erawati and her parents were determined to win over every impediment. The thoughts in the boulevard of my mind were hindered by the sudden announcement of my name. I had a visitor.

"Ma and Appa are not supposed to come today ... maybe it is Nilofer? Have the words escaped my mind and reached her heart?" It felt unreal. With numerous questions boggling my mind, I walked towards the visiting room.

The visiting room was a drab space, with a number of tables with benches placed sufficiently far away from each other. I always felt that the lighting was inadequate and, together with the peeling white paint on the wall, made the room look uninviting. There were two windows that looked out at the pretty gardens. There was heavy surveillance and guarding and, of course, strict time management for the visitors.

That afternoon, the room was unexpectedly empty. In fact, when I first entered, I couldn't find anyone. But soon, my eyes landed on the corner table by the window. My heart stopped beating and my lips trembled. There was an unnerving tingling sensation at the bottom of my stomach.

Ramanuj!

CHAPTER 19

At the sound of my footsteps, he turned to look at me, straight into my eyes. I could not move; my legs were frozen. Tears rolled down my eyes. The last time our eyes had met, we were on that menacing riverside, experiencing the most horrid event of our lives. I vividly remember that look in his eyes, as if it was yesterday.

Ramanuj had grown frail, and his eyes had lost its twinkle. But when he smiled at me, I connected to its warmth like never before. In swift steps, I walked over to him and without letting any thought arise in my mind, I hugged him tight. He reciprocated with passion. We were both crying.

"I am sorry, Ramanuj," I mumbled, unaware of what I was saying. "I am sorry."

Freeing himself from my embrace, he looked at me. "Why are you sorry? It's me who should apologize. And no apology would ever suffice. My one mistake changed your life forever—both our lives! Era ... I am sorry. Sorry for not being able to save you." He wept like a child.

"Nobody could have saved me that fateful day. I was destined to be the Eos of the infernal," I responded firmly. "There are often many layers to life beyond the obvious, and I have visited those forbidden paths. I know life is not what we see. It is much more."

"Era ..."

"Where have you been, Rama? Why didn't you come to see me before? I never admitted this even to myself, but I waited for you every second. Why didn't you embrace me like this before? I craved it so badly. Why Rama, why?"

"Because I was scared to face you. I thought you wouldn't

want to see my face. After all, I couldn't be a worthy partner, Era. I am ashamed of myself."

I looked into his dark eyes. "Rama ... look at me. I have traversed a long journey and a rough one at that. But do you see any negativity in my demeanour? Do you sense bitterness in me?"

"No, Era!"

"That's because I have learnt to appreciate the positives of life. I have seen people go through unimaginable pain and owning every affliction with grace. Life has shaped me, hardened me, and made me discover myself. A protected living would have been great. But then, I would not have known the soreness hidden behind the dolled-up faces of prostitutes or the innocence that was deeply seated in the hearts of the so-called hardened criminals." I smiled, while he just kept looking at me with wonder. "I know life will never be the way we had imagined. Your family will perhaps look at me with abhorrence and so will most of the people of our society." I heaved a sigh and continued, "But I do not regret anything. I respect my journey, and the best part is, even at this tough junction in my wandering life, I have Ma and Appa with me. So nothing else matters—"

"And what about me?" he asked before I could finish.

"You?" I set my eyes on him as tears rolled down his cheeks. My heart was racing. "You are my Eos of the infernal."